SHARED MEMORIES

a novel

GARY L. STUART

Shared Memories

For information about this title or to order other books and/or electronic media, contact the publisher:
Gleason & Wall Publishers
7000 N. 16th Street, Suite 120, PBM 470, Phoenix, AZ 85020
www.garylstuart.com
gary.stuart@garylstuart.com

ISBN: 978-1-7368946-2-0 (print)
         978-1-7368946-3-7 (eBook)

Printed in the United States of America

Cover and Interior design: 1106 Design, Phoenix, AZ

Other Books by Gary L. Stuart

The Ethical Trial Lawyer

The Gallup 14

*Miranda—The Story of America's
Right to Remain Silent*

*Innocent Until Interrogated—The True Story of the
Buddhist Temple Massacre and the Tucson Four*

AIM for the Mayor—Echoes from Wounded Knee

Anatomy of a Confession—The Debra Milke Case

Ten Shoes Up

The Valles Caldera

The Last Stage to Bosque Redondo

*Call Him Mac—Ernest W. McFarland—
The Arizona Years*

Let's Disappear

Emergence

Tracking Tom Horn's Confession

CHAPTER 1

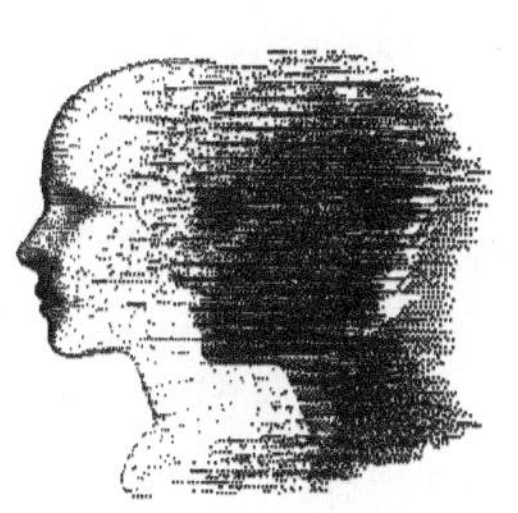

No one knew where Vince, Vivian, or Vinessa were. Dr. Ahmed Estancia, Vinessa's psychiatrist at the Rice University Medical Center, got a handwritten note from her. It was postmarked Auckland, New Zealand, three months after the dismissal of all pending criminal cases. By then the lives of Amherst Pipps and Dish Joandiz had been memorialized by their families in Texas.

The handwritten note read:

Dear Dr. Estancia,

We heard the news from Houston about Julia Baby. We know calling her that must sound unkind, given her violent death. But if there ever was a person who deserved a violent death, it was her. I'm using the royal "we" in this note. You'll understand why. We could not find a psychiatrist in either New Zealand or Australia who knew much about multiplicity, but it is of no consequence. A young counselor, Garrison Venable, who trained in Ireland, has a master's degree. He knows us, and our issues. In fact, he's one of us. We will always think of you kindly. Our business is flourishing. Did we mention to you that it is called Emergence Inc.? We're happy to report that it finds favor in Europe, the UK, and in Australia. We help others in the multiplicity community deal with financial issues, identity issues, and ways to make up for lost time.

Warmest best wishes,

V's

Of course, Dr. Estancia didn't reply to her letter. There was no return address on the envelope, and Vinessa's new location was unknown by anyone in Texas, or in Arizona. Dr. Estancia swiveled his desk chair around to the file cabinet behind his desk. The middle drawer was labeled "Dissociative Identity Disorder Patient Files." Thumbing through alphabetically arrayed hanger-files, he fished out her file. The tab noted, Vivian, Vince, Vinessa—Arizona. He flipped to the rear of the small sheaf of paper-clipped notes and looked again at her registration card.

Patient Name: Vivian Shortfield, aka Vivian Nau, aka Vince (alter state), aka Vinessa (adult chosen first name)

Diagnosis: Dissociative Identity Disorder (DSM-5).

Initial Clinical Assessment: DID—identity disruption—two distinct personality states; marked discontinuity in sense of self and/or agency; changes in affect, behavior, consciousness, memory, perception; cognition intact; sensory-motor function normal; question—dissociative amnesia; question—disruption in autobiographical memory. Likely cause—trauma age nine—lake drowning of playmate.

Treatment—psychotherapy—no RX.

Then he inserted Vinessa's note in the rear of the clipped file, after noting the date, April 15, 2018, in longhand and printing; he wrote, "patient discontinued treatment."

Garrison Venable sat in his car in the Phoenix City Grille's parking lot waiting for his takeout order. As usual, he was listening to 91.5 KJZZ as it rounded off the news about the possibility of Arizona turning blue for the first time since 1952. He was always happy on St. Patrick's Day, and he was determined not to let the gloom of 2020's COVID-19 pandemic spoil his corned beef and cabbage. The litany of new COVID-19 cases was drum rolling across the bottom of his iPhone. Vinessa wanted the salmon cedar plank dinner. He'd ordered the Saint Patty Day special. As the masked waiter came through the double doors on the sidewalk, he heard the incoming text on his phone. Clicking on it, he heard the one-word message. "LEAVE."

He started the engine, shifted into reverse, and backed out, nearly hitting the shiny new Lexis pulling into the space next to him. The befuddled waiter hollered, *Hey, is this yours*, as he moved south to the end of the parking lot and swung out onto 16th Street, causing two cars to bang their horns at him.

No, not now, he thought. We're getting so close.

CHAPTER 2 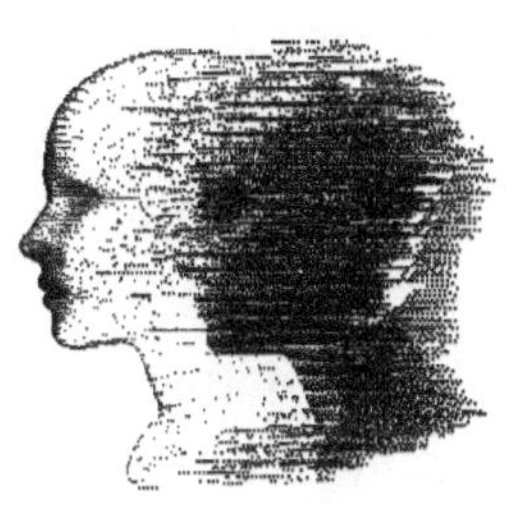

The Desert Mountain Country Club in Carefree was 28.4 miles from the restaurant's parking lot. Garrison knew that because he'd just clocked it coming down from Vinessa's rental home on the fairway. *Bloody hell*, he thought. *Must be cyber,* he guessed, as he made the right turn on Bethany Home to catch the 51 north. She had located him using her *FindMyPhone* app. He used the same app. No contact. She was out of the house, probably walking down 94th Place to the Clubhouse. *Strange*, he thought. Their code, LEAVE, was as ominous for them as it was innocuous to anyone that might gain access to their texts. It meant she was under surveillance. Why was she out of the house? And why, at this time of night, on the ninth fairway?

Drumming his right hand on the steering wheel, he reached out, punched in the four-number code at the main entrance, and watched the eight-foot-tall, shuttered steel door slide slowly open. *What's taking so long?* It was a four-minute drive from there up to the house. Most of the other houses he passed were dark—owned as second homes by snowbirds who'd show up after Christmas and spend the spring golfing and drinking at the posh country club. Swinging right onto the brick driveway, he punched the far right button under the mirror to open the oversized garage door. Her car was there. *Goddammit, not now, not now!*

After banging on the door to the main house for a minute and not getting an answer, he went through the side gate leading to the pool area and the small casita in back where he lived. He could see through the floor-to-ceiling glass at the rear of the main house that she wasn't in the kitchen, the movie room, or rear hallway.

"Vinessa, where you?"

"She's gone," the husky voice said from the casita on the far side of the pool.

He froze. The voice sounded only distantly familiar, but the next instant, he knew who it was. They'd met once, almost a year ago. The ornate casita door was wide open and he could see inside all the way to the back wall. The overhead lights were on, as was the fan he never used. Vince was sitting in his webbed office chair, tapping away on his keyboard. Over his shoulder, he mumbled to the monitor, "Now there you are, motherfucker, you belong to me now."

"Vince," he said to the black leather jacket as he flew through the door, "where is she?"

"Gone," Vince said, without looking back. "Ain't you glad to see me? You still comptrolling her? What 'n freaking hell is a comptroller, anyhow?"

Garrison wondered for just a moment whether this was the same Vince he'd encountered in Australia almost a year ago. Then, he'd worn a heavy coat and an Australian shearling Cossack hat. Now in sunny Arizona, he sported a thin A-shirt, walking shorts, and Skechers. His angular, small-boned body gave him a reedy look. Whereas his sister, Vinessa, looked willowy, her little brother seemed outright skeletal.

Vince held his left hand up and waved one of Garrison's business cards at him. He'd only experienced Vince that one time in Australia. He hadn't changed—compulsive, devious, and needy. Garrison had hesitated then to diagnose Vinessa's so-called little brother as either bipolar or OCD, and he resisted the temptation again. *Vinessa needs him.*

"Like it says, on my card, I'm the comptroller. I take care of the company's investments and budgeting," Garrison answered.

Vince swung the swivel chair around and faced him like a bully in a playground. He thought his sneer alone was enough to command attention. He waited with his arms outstretched, palms up, and swinging his upper body from back to front. Garrison ignored the posturing.

"OK, Vince. Nice to see you too. Let's cut the BS. I assume she's out of time. You're here. That's how it works, right? She feels threatened, I mean really threatened, not just scared. You show up. When the threat is controlled, you poof away like the morning fog over the Irish Sea. Right?"

"Yeah, yeah, Mr. Irishman. You think being Irish is special, I know. Is that why she hired you to comptroll shit in the real world, the one *we* live in, but *you* only study?

She said you are her freakin' therapist twice a week and our company's comptroller the rest of the time. You need to remember the company belongs to me when she's out."

"Technically, you're right," Garrison said, hoping it might calm him enough to explain the LEAVE text he'd received from Vinessa thirty-five minutes ago. *Was it to him, or herself?*

"Fuck's that? I asked you what a comptroller is—means shit to me."

The only other time Garrison had engaged Vince in Australia was after Vinessa became one of his patients at the multiplicity clinic. Like all DID clinics, the treatment of choice was individual psychotherapy—preferably weekly. Drugs were rarely prescribed except for narrowly defined depression or acute anxiety. Group therapy was never successful and, on the few occasions where it was tried, resulted in patients going "out of time" during group sessions. He knew he had to be careful with Vince because the phrase "going out of time" might have enraged him. Psychiatrists and therapists used "going out of time" with patients to explain the mental transfer from the dominant personality state to the alter personality state. Of course, they'd say, you are just one person, not two separate people, but when you "go out of time" your alter state takes over so you're not threatened by any trauma or mental disassociation.

He spent a year with her, and developed a strong clinical relationship and a professional friendship. Then, last summer year she hired him as the Emergence Incorporated comptroller. They were inconsistent endeavors, mental health counseling and financial management, but he was good at both.

"OK, Vince, I'll answer your question first. A comptroller is a management-level position. Vinessa hired me to work for Emergence Inc. Technically I'm responsible for supervising the quality of accounting and financial reporting. But I'm not the company treasurer. She is both CEO and treasurer. Bit of an odd mix, like mixing Jamison's Irish whiskey and water. But it's her company. She lets me live in this casita. She lives in the main house across the pool. It's Platonic, in case you were wondering. I do the books and help her with identity issues. How about answering my question now—where is she?"

"Fuck if I know. I'm here, so she's not. That's how multiplicity works, right? Can you account for that?" he asked, snickering at his own pun.

"I can. Something terrified her within the last hour. That's my therapist account. What are you doing on my computer?"

"Fixing what terrified her. Ransomware. If I don't fix it, you will be out of a job and she will be writing a big ransom check to get our company data back. It's not just her company, you know."

Garrison knew more about the financial consequences of ransomware than Vince would ever know. But this was not the time to educate him.

"Are you on the local drive, Vince? And was Vinessa on it when she went out of time?"

"Shit yeah, I'm on 'C,' but I'm using Firefox to get to TOR. You know about TOR right?"

"Yes, a little. It's an online relay point. Some of our data—that is, Emergence Incorporated's data—is on an encrypted VPN on the Deep Web. Ransomware can't reach that data because it's already encrypted, not to mention impossible to find."

"Okay, doc," Vince said, flipping his long hair in annoyance, "you get a C-plus in software, but I think Vinessa freaked out because the Ukrainian bastards might have locked up our financial data like you're supposed to be in charge of."

"No, I doubt that. Do you see the logo on the far right of the task bar on the monitor? The blue and white target with the blue indent in the upper right corner?"

"Yeah, what's that?"

"Open it, you'll see."

Vince double clicked and a new screen opened—*Citrix Workspace*. "Citrix? Never been there, but I think it's some kind of businessmen's crap."

"No, Vince, it's a digital workspace software platform. We have an account there. All corporate financial data is right there, not on the local drive. It's a private cloud, known to the world, but inside an account impossible to encrypt because it's already encrypted, by us. And impossible to lock down. We have a cyber-firewall against those sixteen-year-old bandits overseas. We have nothing that needs protection on my local C-drive. Even my email is lodged on an offsite Microsoft Exchange server. Everything there is encrypted, even while in transit."

"Well, my man! How about you don't tell Vinessa that? I kinda like being here. Vivian and I went to school here, not in Phoenix, but in Cranston, a crappy little town south of here. She tell you about our white trash trailer? Dad was among the living in those days."

"OK, Vince. Did anything else happen to scare Vinessa?"

He didn't answer. He swung around in the swivel chair, got up, grabbed his backpack, and walked out the glass sliding door to the pool. Garrison watched him as far as the block wall running alongside the garage until he turned the corner. He shut down his computer and walked outside across the pool to the Lanai area. He could see into the kitchen. Vinessa was looking into the refrigerator with her back to him. She was one of those women who at thirty had matured perfectly. But today her face was locked tight with whitish lines around her forehead and crow's feet on the edges of both eyes. She turned around, saw him, and gave a little wave. Walking around the pool, he met her at the back door.

"Oh, Garrison, I think I fell asleep or something. Weren't you going to get us takeout dinner at the Phoenix City Grille?"

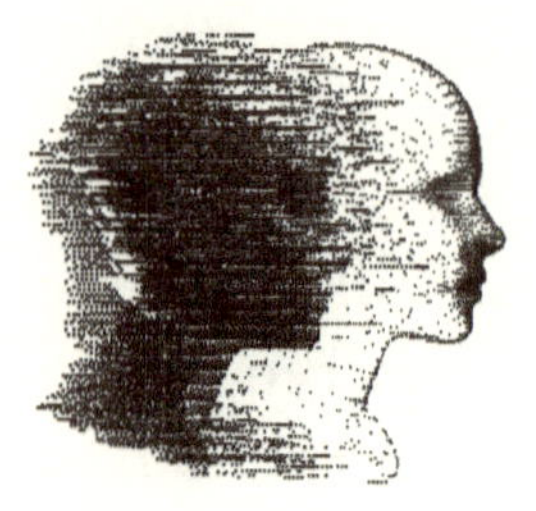# CHAPTER 3

Garrison said she should go to bed. They could talk in the morning about her time out. She smiled and agreed. He watched her walk down the hallway to the master suite. He made himself a mayo and cheese sandwich and took it back to the casita. After six hours of fitful sleep he woke up just before sunrise. In shorts and t-shirt, he logged back on to confirm their data was safe. Whatever happened last night didn't come from the bug-a-boo ransomware that freaked out Vivian and sprouted Vince.

"I timed out, last night, didn't I?" she asked as she sipped her homemade latte with sugar-free vanilla and nonfat milk. She'd made him one too.

"Yes, when I got back after getting your LEAVE text, Vince was here—in my casita office—thinking the problem was a cyber-attack—ransomware, he thought."

"No, that wasn't it. Something much worse. I got a call on the house line—the damn *house line*—how did they find that?"

"Who?"

"The nurse at the COVID testing site we went to day before yesterday. I thought she was calling to say I tested positive and I just freaked out. She said right away that I was not positive, I mean no COVID, but then she asked about my parents, brothers, sisters, relatives, and anyone *I cared about*. I didn't know what to say at first, you know? My parents are dead, but what about you? My alters, Vivian and Vince, don't count—I don't have it, they don't have it. Right? But still it just kept hounding my so-called *dissociated identity disordered* brain after she hung up. Who am I? Really?"

Garrison knew from their many therapy sessions that Vinessa, like most *DID* patients in their early thirties, was perpetually fearful about the past. He gave her an uh-uh, and sipped his latte as she continued.

"We've been pretending for so long. My true identity is in doubt, at least in my own mind. I'm hardly ever Vivian any more. And when Vince is here, I hate it. His potty mouth, his slouching and spitting. He's just disgusting. Here's the real thing. I realized that for me, COVID-19 *is multiple*. MULTIPLE! Do you think Vince would wear a mask, or keep his distance from other people? He could get COVID-19 immediately. What happens to me then? I mean, you saw it last night, didn't you? I sent our LEAVE code because I was near timing out. You came home. Vince was here. I only came back when—somehow, I never know how—I heard your voice from the casita. *I'm* terrified of COVID-19, but *we* aren't. I hate it!"

"Vinessa, you are the person sitting here talking to me. Alters don't count. They don't get sick or COVID-19."

"But Garrison, don't you see? It's not just us anymore either. We have a real company now—Emergence Incorporated. If I get COVID, what happens to the company? Does the company survive my death if COVID-19 knocks on *our* front door tomorrow? Have you thought about that? Vivian could not run the company; she's too young. She's who I used to be. Vince? Can you imagine him running the company, actually helping other people? He is my bodyguard, at least emotionally. I know he's not real. But the world out there has seen him, talked to him, and, well you know all that."

"Yes, I do know Vince. I talked to him yesterday in the casita. And I know what he did for you, while he *was* you in Texas two years ago. He hired a lawyer named Travis Danders. He did some terrible things to that woman, Julia Santerra-Evans, who murdered your father in Washington, DC, five years ago. You told me all of that in one of our therapy sessions. Of course, you were hypothesized at the time, but you carefully explained all of it to me. Your autobiographical memory is intact—the only DID patient I ever heard of to have that gift—the gift of knowing who you are and what happens when you time out. Your company is safe from Vince."

"No, I'm not sure that's right. I know Vince and Vivian did the first legal research for the company. Then, when we hired you to be our comptroller, you and Vince worked together to bury the company inside two corporate layers in Delaware and Nevada. It's a perfectly legal company, and its true owners are not discoverable, even in a court of law. That's what both of you told me. I even remember some of your actual words. You said there's only one owner, even though all three of us created it. Is that why Vince was here last night? You said he was using your computer."

He raised his hands up in a give-up gesture.

"Yes, Vinessa, I did say that, both in a clinic environment and as your financial advisor. But Vince was on the wrong track. No one can find out corporate ownership except by public records. Your family, excuse me, your *community*, created interlocking LLCs in two states that preclude public knowledge of member ownership. The exception, as I've explained before, is a warrant from a federal court."

"Yes, now I remember," she said, speaking through clenched teeth. "But can someone get that—a warrant? Can't the FBI do that?"

"Maybe, but they would have to have probable cause—that's the legal word for it. You talked to a lawyer in Sydney before you started our therapy sessions there. Did you ever talk to him about any of this?"

"No, but he did help Vince, or was it Vivian, I forget, to allow us to accept new identity clients in Australia. We did the same thing in London. Remember?"

"Yes, and it's even harder there to open court records that are protected by law. I think you should consult a good lawyer here in Arizona, but through me. I'm another layer of protection for you. I have a new idea for Emergence Inc."

"Do you mean a criminal lawyer? We haven't committed any crimes. Vince was sure about that. I looked it up too. It's perfectly legal—our whole identity withdrawal program was legal. All we did then, and are still doing now, is help people create new identities for themselves. We know some are hiding because of legal things, but most are just multiplicity people who need a fresh start without a troubling history coming back to haunt, or taunt, or whatever."

"No, Vinessa, I don't mean that kind of lawyer. I think we need a commercial transaction lawyer, one who knows business organizations and tax law. Our members that we create new identities for are safe from the world. But COVID-19 makes the world more dangerous. I've been thinking about those members. Most of their assets are under the new names and identities we built for them. What happens to those assets when they die? Emergence Incorporated took in almost half a million dollars last year in gross revenue and this year we have to change our IRS filings. That's one reason I recommended you lease this house here in Arizona—to establish residency."

"But the lease is not in my name—you arranged the lease through one of the LLCs in Nevada. I don't understand how being an Arizona resident impacts my tax status."

"And that, my dear, is exactly why you hired me. I did corporate tax returns in Texas before I moved to Australia four years ago. Remember? I was a tax accountant before I became a mental health counselor. I know how to cook books and soothe minds, right? You laughed at that when I first told you my job description."

"Okay, Garrison. You're right again. Go find us a commercial whatever lawyer."

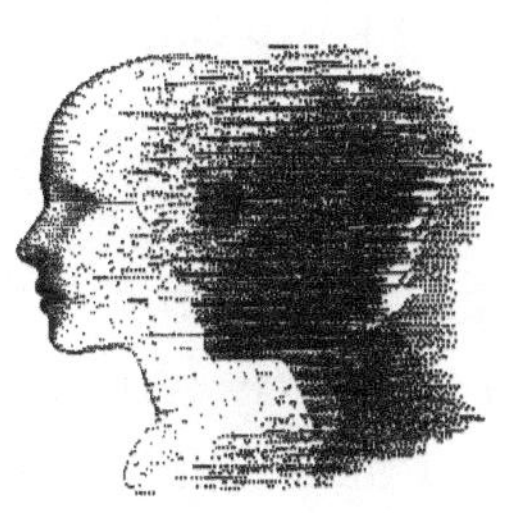

CHAPTER 4

He spent two days making lists, reading catch-up statutes, and checking credentials on the Arizona Bar Association website. All of that helped, but now with his notes organized in a Microsoft OneNote digital file, he could see a plan. It was largely based on recreating what the infamous Bernard Madoff had done, *before* they caught him. Madoff's downfall was that he was too human, lived an open life, and never even tried to hide his identity, or his money. Garrison thought he'd discovered a way for a company to do what Madoff did, without getting caught. A new LLC that was virtual, digital, and erasable at the stroke of a delete key on his personal computer.

The first meeting with Alberta Sundersen in Tempe was pure vanilla. He and Vinessa used newly made-up names, Mr. Sanch Rosener and his nearly deaf wife, Eta Rosener. They met the prematurely graying Ms. Sundersen in her office, not far from the ASU campus. Based on her

Arizona State Bar credentials she struck Garrison as a perfect choice. She'd graduated from a night law school in San Francisco twenty years ago, failed the California bar exam, but passed in Arizona. She took a job as in-house counsel for a bank, which lasted a year, then worked for a private two-lawyer firm that did transactional work for small to medium sized businesses in Pima County. Then, eight years ago, the Supreme Court gave her a two-year suspension for negligently handling a complex business transaction that cost her client $50,000. The state bar file indicated the core problem was alcoholism. She spent too much time drunk and not enough time with the client to prevent the default on most of its business debt. Now she was sober, born again, with a renewed law license, but not very many clients. She shared space in a thirty-year old building.

"Good morning, Mr. Rosener, it's good to meet you in person. And you too, Mrs. Rosener. Now, we've talked on the phone, and I understand you want to form a new business company in Arizona. What kind of business?"

Garrison said, "Ms. Sundersen, before we tell you anything, we want to make sure what we tell you is confidential. We retained a lawyer back in Iowa who listened to us, and then said he didn't want us as clients because we couldn't pay his fee. Can we talk about confidentiality and fees first?"

"If you like," she said. "But I cannot give you an estimate of my fee without knowing what you want me to do. I can tell you this first meeting is absolutely confidential. Even if I don't take you as a client, our ethical rules prohibit me from telling anyone what you say to me, or I say to you. That's the lawyer's duty of confidentiality. It's the same in all states, including Iowa. I'm sorry to hear about your experience there."

"Okay, that makes us feel better. There's something else. I looked at your state bar record and know you lost your license but are now fully licensed. I actually went to the bar office, and they let me read a part of your file. It said you abandoned your client on a business transaction and that you admitted your mistakes and were in an alcoholism program. We know a good deal about that, alcoholism I mean. We are both recovering and have been sober for seven years. We believe in redemption with the Lord. Can you assure us of your faith and your sobriety?"

"Well, Mr. Rosener, I thank you for telling me that. I have made a habit of telling new clients about my past but not usually this early in the lawyer-client relationship. I made serious mistakes because I was an alcoholic. It made me a bad lawyer for a while. But I'm sober now, and I give thanks to my Lord and Savior every day for that."

"There's another thing," Garrison said, looking at Vinessa. "Eta had her troubles with drinking, but not as serious as me. I was a fall-down kind of drunk. She never got that far. But we want you to know about something else that is important to us. She has been diagnosed as suffering from a dissociative identity disorder. Do you know what that is?"

"Dissociative identity? Not sure what that means. I was never good at science and my only mental health problem was drinking. Can you explain?"

"Well, it's too complicated and would take up a lot of time. Why don't you google it later? We're telling you about it because it relates to the kind of business we're in and to the corporate entity that we think we need at this stage of our business. You see, we're in the identity business, actually the changing-your-identity business."

"Goodness, Mr. Rosener, I have to say I'm not sure what you mean. You're in the *identity changing* business?"

Garrison shuffled in his seat and looked back and forth from Vinessa to the lawyer before he answered.

"Yes, let me explain it this way. You know about the federal witness protection program, don't you?"

"I've heard of it, but only in newspapers. It's not my field of law—criminal cases. How does it relate to your business?"

"Ms. Sundersen, this is why we wanted to make sure what we say to you is protected, is confidential, and that you'll never tell anyone about us. I'll answer your question, but I want you to say it again. What we say is confidential, right?"

"Yes, sir, it is. As long as you're not using my legal services to commit a crime. Then the confidentiality rule does not apply."

"All right then. What we're doing is perfectly legal. We're only doing privately what the federal government does openly. It offers witness protection to people who testify in criminal cases. Those people know that if they went on about their lives with their real names in the same way they did before testifying, their lives would be in danger. The US Marshal's office provides new identity documents, new places to live, some money to start a new life, and a promise to watch over them after their testimony in court is given and the bad guys are in prison. That' it. What we do is similar, only it's done privately. No public help. No public money. We create new identities, new lives, and new places to live for people who want to disappear. We have a new idea about how to expand our business. It's with a different kind of identity changing—a family trust. Can you help us with that?"

"You want to create a trust for your family, is that right?"

"No, not exactly. We want to create family trusts for our community. It's a community of people who want anonymity. They want to be invisible. And mostly, they want new lives. I have done my research, but I'm not a lawyer. What we want to know from you is whether you can write trust documents that ensure anonymity, both for the people in the trust and the money held in trust?"

Ms. Sundersen turned out to be an ideal lawyer, at least from Garrison's perspective. It would take three months. Garrison and Vinessa, with help from her, created a master family trust in Arizona under fake names, with fake assets, in a fake bank. Garrison negotiated a flat fee—$2,000. Half now and half when she finished the documents. She never suspected a thing. She did her job, giving all the operative documents to a family that didn't exist—the Sanch and Eta Rosener family—names made up by Garrison and Vinessa. Emergence Inc. was now in the business of creating not just LLCs to hide identities, but family trusts to hide money.

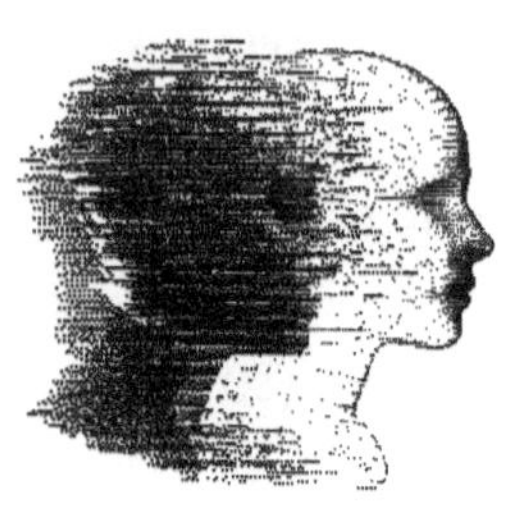# CHAPTER 5

Once they got the files in Word from Ms. Sundersen's law clerk, Garrison used the forms to create his first family trust. For demonstrations he named it *The Paul and Teresa Barnum Family Trust*. He made two copies and, after breakfast, explained to Vinessa how it would work.

"Oh, Vinessa," he said with a grandiose wave of the hand at the twelve-page printed Word document on the table next to the *New York Times*. "This marks a new era in your career of helping multiplicity communities deal with the stress and fear COVID-19 has brought to everyone, especially those who, like you, Vivian, and Vince, are living under new chosen identities. I'm sure your dad would be very proud of this."

"I trust you, Garrison, but to be honest, I still don't understand how these trusts work and why multiplicity people would pay us to create them. I mean, we're not bankers or investment experts. I know this document looks impressive what with all the whereas and wherefore language, but what does it really do?"

"Want more coffee?" Garrison asked. He knew this would be stressful since Vinessa never enjoyed legal or tax minutiae. She waved him off.

"No thanks. Just be patient with me; I'll probably ask stupid questions."

Garrison took in a deep breath, knowing this conversation was pivotal. He clenched his jaw line and began the sell.

"All right, here's the main thing, Vinessa. You created Emergence Inc. so that people could get new identities—actually new names, addresses, social security numbers, bank accounts. In addition, people who want to really disappear need erasers and scrubbers of all kinds. They are erasing their past lives and writing new ones under new identities. These people have to trust you to make their past lives invisible. They paid your company a substantial fee to do the intricate work it takes to get new documents that prove they are who they 'say they are.' Your motto for three years has been, *You Are Who You Say You Are.* That simple announcement makes all of them feel safe in their new lives. And as a benefit to them, we created a membership to continue to help them with new problems, like changing car titles, getting new mortgages, and finding online banking where personal presence is unnecessary. For that, every member pays us a nominal dues payment of twenty-five dollars a month. Now that we've got close to three hundred members, we get about $7,500 per month, plus the fees we earn for setting up their new documents. That earned the company $562,000 net, year before last, and was up eleven percent last year. Now, let me ask you a simple question. Why do these people pay you, actually your company, that much money every month?"

"I don't know. They are all like us. Is that it? All multiplicity people who need new lives for myriad reasons. Each has a different reason to come to us."

"Vinessa, you were right in the beginning. But not now. They come to Emergence Incorporated and pay you monthly because they *trust* you. They needed a new life—you helped them get it. They have new small problems every once in a while, and they ask you what to do. You always have solutions for them. But as they become successful in their new lives, they accumulate things. Houses, cars, bank accounts, and investments. Most have assets they want to leave to their children when they pass on. But they know that will be difficult because we have created new identities for them. How will a probate court deal with the fake lives we've created for them? I can tell you what most people with decent assets do. They completely avoid probate court. They pass on whatever they have through a legal document called a living trust. It does not go through probate. The trustees in the trust pass on the trust assets in strict accordance with the written terms. That's our new service for multiplicity people—living trusts to keep hidden everything they have already kept secret, thanks to us."

Vinessa pinched her bottom lip. He knew she would become emotional when she felt conflicted.

"I'm not sure, Garrison. We don't personally know these people. I mean, I've talked on the phone with one or two family leaders. But that's all. We can help our members because we share histories with them and know how frightful life can be. Take this COVID nightmare. Who can tell the future anymore?"

"Actually, my dear, you're arguing *for* my idea. Who can tell the future indeed! No one can. All the more reason to find ways to protect what you have, make sure it gets into the right hands, and above all find someone who knows exactly who we are. We are who we say we are. Emergence Incorporated is the answer, not the future, just the answer to a future no one can predict."

"Well, I have to say this. Did you come up with this solution as a therapist or as an accountant?"

"Both. We have to create the future of your company by planning for it. And we have to be safe and mentally healthy in the present because otherwise COVID-19 will drive us crazy."

"OK, Garrison, give me the elevator speech. How will a family trust help our people?"

He reached into his file folder and withdrew a single piece of paper with one double-spaced paragraph. "I drafted this yesterday. Let me read it to you."

```
Your Emergence Inc. Family Trust will
hold, invest, and distribute your
assets after you die or become inca-
pacitated. You will be the grantor of
the trust. It is revocable by you at
any time for any reason. The trust
will own the assets but you can use
the assets in the trust just as you've
done all your life. You retain full
```

control. You appoint our company as
the trustee, just as you would do for
your checking account at your local
bank. You can close the account or add
to it. You can change the assets in
the trust. Unlike a checking account,
a trust account can hold houses, cars,
jewelry, art, or intellectual property. You can disperse real or personal property in any way you want.
The beneficiaries can be changed by
you. The *Emergence Inc. Family Trust*
will grow at a modest rate—we project an annual growth rate of two to
three percent. It is not taxed. You
simply include the trust results in
your personal tax returns.

Frowning, she said, "That sounds too good to be true. How could we promise a steady return of three percent?"

"Because that's exactly what any bank will pay these days. And besides, it's just a projection. All we're really doing for our members is moving their money from ordinary banks into trust accounts, which we oversee as trustees. The trust accounts will pay around three percent. We take out some for expenses and reinvest the rest for them, inside the living trust itself. And we tell them every year how well they are doing and help them write directions to the trustees, that's us, on how to pay the money out to relatives when the grantors—our clients—die. It's what people who live public lives do all the time to avoid probate and keep their personal names off the public record."

"Well, I guess that makes sense. But I still don't see why they need this trust."

"They need it because none of our people want to go to probate court and divulge their names, addresses, or details about their lives. Vinessa, don't you see this? They don't want to take an oath in court and tell the truth. They can't give testimony to a judge. Would you do that? What would you say when the judge says, 'State your name, please'? This way, through a family trust, they protect their assets, and they protect their new lives from prying eyes, judges, courtrooms, everything! All of it is done privately, just like they are leading the rest of their new lives—the ones we created for them."

"Oh, Garrison, I'm sure you're right. I guess I still don't see how *we* fit in—we are not lawyers. Don't we need lawyers to write these family trusts?"

"No, we don't. We have the forms already, thanks to Alberta Sundersen in Tempe. We can do it all now. Our people can avoid any legal challenges to how they want their assets dispersed. It's airtight legally."

"I didn't understand what you said about taxes."

"That's another big advantage over a simple will. It can limit exposure to estate taxes. But that's not the biggest selling point."

"Which is?" Vinessa asked as she pushed her shoulders back and lifted her chin up.

"It's simple. We can prepare hundreds of new family trusts based on the documents we got from Alberta Sundersen. There are a few other documents we need, like transfer instruction forms. We'll do the filing ourselves.

Transferring ownership of assets is easy, if you have the right forms. Just think about it, Vinessa. You have given hundreds of multiplicity families privacy and security in their new lives. Peace of mind is next in line. We can offer that with a family trust, in easy times, or in horrific times, like now."

With that, Vinessa nodded her head. Garrison went back to the casita to prepare the first announcement to dues-paying members of Emergence Inc.

CHAPTER 6

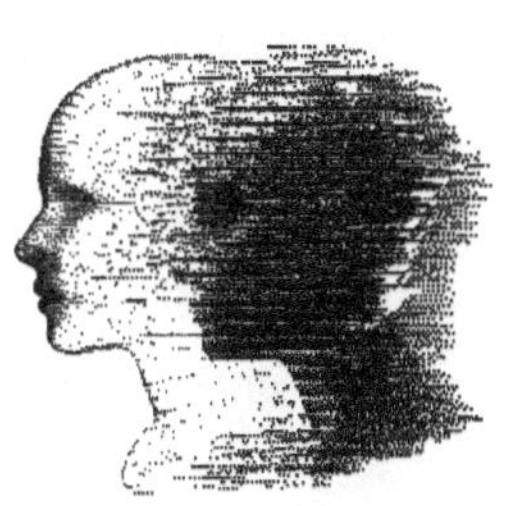

Garrison's importance to Vinessa, her alters, and to their business story was essential. She helped her clients become new people, some of them very rich. They loved the ability Emergence Inc. gave them. It protected them from their past lives and enabled them to be new in every sense of the word. Without him, Vinessa might not have retained her role in Vivian's life—she was the new Vivian. Vince was not—he was an alter—available when Vivian felt threatened. In her teens, Vivian was absorbable at any moment. Poof, Vince is back, and just in time. In her twenties, Vivian grew into Vinessa, a more confident, less threatened Vivian.

What none of them knew for sure was how intricately Garrison had blended himself into their ongoing therapy, financial success, and transmutability. Vinessa suspected that Garrison knew their lives and problems so well because he himself had something to hide, or someone he either hated or feared.

Unlike Vivian/Vince/Vinessa, Garrison felt comfortable and in control of his own life, until he wasn't. Then he acted out, sometimes like a petulant child, and later like an angry adult.

Vinessa buried her suspicion about Garrison just as she had always done with Vince and Vivian. Like nearly all multiplicity people, she assumed other people were who they said they were—not alters. Over time, once Vince ended the nightmare in Houston, Texas, with Julia Baby, Vinessa's life had been continuous therapy, first with Dr. Estancia in Texas and then with Garrison in Australia.

Garrison's path differed. He had a mother, a twin brother, and no father—that's how he remembered his childhood. His mother divorced his father five years after he and his twin, Gilbert, were born. She kept him. His dad got Gilbert. The little farm town in Iowa was aghast that divorcing parents separated twin boys the same way they did the family cars. Mom got the Honda Civic and Dad got the F-150. When Dad and Gilbert visited, twice a year, the twins thought they were looking into a mirror. Except that Garrison had an attitude, and Gilbert was tongue-tied. After their weekend visits, Dad took Gilbert back to British Columbia and the fish-packing plant where he worked.

In his early teens, Garrison was diagnosed with DMDD—disruptive mood dysregulation disorder—by a Denver, Colorado, pediatric psychiatrist. The diagnosis is made based on frequent, persistent, severe temper outbursts out of proportion to the situation. There was a developmental context—persistent angry/irritable moods between the outbursts.

His single working mother, a nursing assistant in a government-operated nursing home, was afraid of him. She said he seemed to know his own condition better than the doctors who examined him. She told the doctor that her teenage son was a kind Garrison one day and a mean Garrison the next. The doctor prescribed Risperidone, which his mother gave him for a little over a year. Then, she thought, he just seemed to grow out of the temper tantrums.

The year after his diagnosis, he turned seventeen and his mother simply disappeared. He did not report her missing, and he left Colorado shortly after her disappearance. At eighteen, he took a job as a children's playtime counselor on an Australian cruise ship for nine months before returning to the United States and going to school in Chicago. He never spoke of his childhood, parents, or Colorado again.

His BSBA in finance from a state university gave him the experience he needed to resolve financial irregularities. His first job with a credit union failed, and he went back to school. His MA in counseling from an online university in Chicago gave him the necessary credentials to do both clinical work in a group setting, and provide ongoing therapy. He'd liked Australia during his nine-month cruise ship job. So with two new degrees, he left Illinois and found a clinical job in Sydney.

It's rare for anyone afflicted with a childhood diagnosis like disruptive mood disorder to show symptoms as an adult. Garrison gained confidence as a children's playtime counselor and forgot all about the imaginary friend he had in junior high school. He knew she wasn't real, but for him, she was a much-needed barrier to the bullying of seventh and eighth graders.

He'd named her Toozie because he imagined she was two years older than he was. In junior high he read books about female anatomy and sex and then pretended to teach her about masturbation, premature ejaculation, and other things too delicate to talk about with real people. He thought of himself as asexual and above all that nasty stuff. He jettisoned Toozie in his sophomore year of high school, but maintained his insistence in college that he was asexual. He pleasured himself once a week and no one ever guessed. Or cared. He liked that.

In one of his first therapy sessions in Australia with Vinessa, he had coached her on what he said was the essence of living with her condition.

"It's more," he told her, "than merely accepting multiplicity. It's the existential awareness of joy and self-fulfillment. It's 'self' in your mind and body. You know, Vinessa, don't you that people have different understandings of what it means to experience this 'more than one' life you're living? In some cultures, what you're experiencing every day was seen as sacred. In other cultures, it was blasphemy. In Salem you might have been seen as a witch. In Athens as a goddess. And in Hollywood as normal. Multiplicity people often have day-to-day experiences that vary widely. Some are extremely stressful and life threatening. Others are thrilling and life enhancing. Your own experience is full of examples at both extremes. Most important in your case is this simple equation. Do you see these *selves* outside of your body as people you can talk to? If not, is that because you choose not to talk to them?"

As he recalled it, her answer was not an answer. She just said, "It's none of your business."

He could remember how satisfied he felt when softly arguing with her about the transient nature of multiplicity. When she came to him from Dr. Estancia in Houston, she saw her condition as temporary. He worked hard to disabuse her of that notion, pushing her to a longer term, "Because," he said, "you would miss out on so much by just being yourself, your former self, all the time."

Like most patients, she could easily see the bad and had no confidence in the good of multiplicity. For her it was confusing to become aware of the many ways people can understand experiences of multiplicity. As they moved forward in a clinical setting, he helped her to see the power of using multiplicity to connect a diversity of meanings and experiences. With the new venture of family trusts under the banner of Emergence Incorporated, he could see riches for himself. But she could see only the good that might come to others.

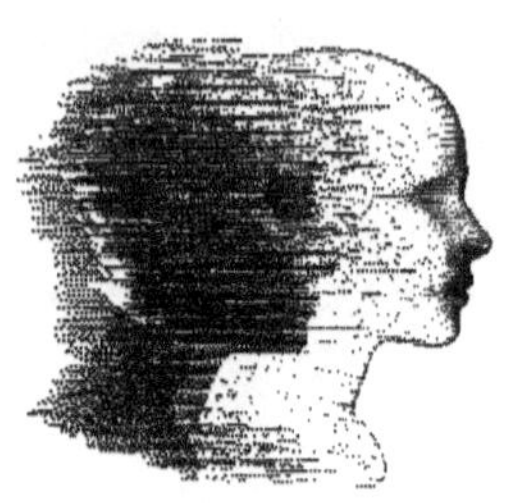

CHAPTER 7

In his therapeutic role, Garrison Venable had always wondered whether it was possible to manipulate a patient's experiential state. He'd researched it and could find no suggestion that a dominant personality state could, *on purpose*, move into or out of an alter state. But the research was replete with the reality that many DID patients alternated back and forth in ways that suggested they had some control—at least in receding from an alter state back to the essential dominant state. All credible research sources agreed on the basic premise of the diagnosis—the patient's lack of awareness that a different identity existed.

Multiplicity people didn't have *more* than one personality. To the contrary they had *less* than one personality. That is why the name for the disorder was changed from the old *multiple personality disorder* to the new *dissociative identity disorder*. In most clinical settings the disorder could be traced to a response to some physical or sexual abuse in childhood. In those cases, afflicted people escaped from, at least in their minds, their abusers. Even if that was the original motivating psychological factor, it did not explain why or how the disorder continued in later life.

Garrison thought it began as a coping mechanism and evolved into an expanding defense to stress. And ultimately he thought that some patients preferred the safer state of an alter to the dangerous state of the dominant personality. That explained why Vivian sometimes lived an enchanted life as Vinessa, and other times retreated to the safety of Vince. She was non-confrontational. He was in your face.

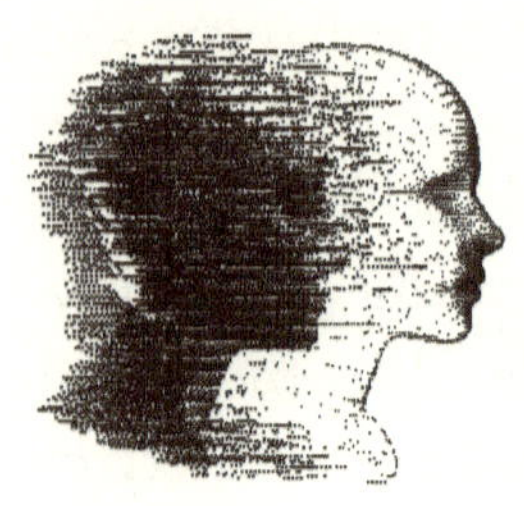# CHAPTER 8

Garrison's new iPhone 6 Health Watch buzzed at him at 5:15 am. He couldn't quite see the screen on his wrist but it seemed to be an email. As he swung his legs out of bed, he got that vague dizzy sense; something was amiss. Turning on the bedside light and reaching for his glasses, the feeling went from unease to teeth gritting. Someone was using his office computer remotely.

More as a calming device than dental hygiene, he forced himself to brush his teeth before pulling on a T-shirt and sweat pants. He padded down the hall to the office at the rear of the house. The second he opened the door, he heard the high-pitched voice he'd come to dread.

"Yo, Garrison. You got my good morning email, but I don't see no steaming coffee in your hand. I said black coffee with two sugars, right?"

"Vince, you have no right to even be in my office not to mention using my computer. How did you open it?"

"Hey, you outta be thanking my sorry ass for the hack. Using an Australian zip code for your logon pin ain't' safe, my man. How you expect me to help you slither your way onto the Dark Web, by making me work for, say, three four minutes to crack your code? Shit man, you're pathetic."

"Australia does not have zip codes, Vince. They have four-digit postal codes, Vince. Please move away from my computer, Vince!"

Garrison's earlier experiences with Vince had been manageable. He'd been fearful that Vince might show up after his long talk with Vinessa. Now that his fear was realized, he needed to find out how to use the smug little hacker without giving him anything that would encourage his presence. He had an irritating habit of picking his nose when he took his hand off the mouse. *I have to make this personality state work for me, not get in my way,* Garrison thought as he switched on the overhead lights in his office. He got the reaction he'd hoped for.

"Dude, why you gotta shine that bright light on me? You're busting my chops. Ain't no accident I'm here, dude. Without me, you're chopped liver. She sent me. To get you guys into the Dark Web. Shit, man. Maybe we outta be down two levels. Member I taught you that, right? There's the Surface Web for plain people who ain't qualified to penetrate beyond Google, Mozilla, and Edge. Then, underneath, there's the Dark Web. Deeper down, way deeper, there's the Deep Web, man. You with me?"

"Vince," Garrison said, trying to sound merely inquisitive, "give me a refresher, will you?"

"All you gotta do is ask, dude. Here's the thing. Reason the US of A military gave us three levels in the Internet is so we can access data different ways, you know what I mean? You got your Surface Web, your Deep Web, and my favorite sink hole—the Dark Web."

Right, Vince, but tell me again why we don't just have one Internet, for everyone?"

"Cuz, my man, pissants can't navigate below the Surface Web. I told you that before. The top layer, for all pissants, has search engines—you call 'em browsers. They have indexed the whole Surface Web so when you type some lame shit like used cars or new movies, sites pop up. One layer down, in the Deep Web, there are no friggin' search engines. No kiss-ass browsers. You want to navigate down there you have to do computer work, like filling out forms, knowing about specific content, and logging into a specific set of content pages."

"Right, Vince. That's where our Emergence data is, right?"

"Yeah, mostly, our stuff is encrypted and housed on the Dark Web. Down there you need special software, like TOR. I told you about that, remember? Down there the dark knights and filthy females dwell like criminals. Down there it's all about levels of the highest level of encryption and anonymity. Kinda like Vinessa's obsession with anonymity, ya know?"

"Right, I know about anonymity and besides that . . ."

Putting the side of his left thumb on his lower lip, and whispering "shhhh," Vince used the index finger on his right hand and slowly tapped out the lowercase letters in uppercase on the screen, "a-n-o-n-y-m-o-u-s-l-y."

Garrison got the hint and lowered his voice.

"Vince, our members live anonymously. And you're right we need to protect that for them. I can do the legal drafting, but she's right in bringing you in. I cannot conceal our online footprint using commercial browsers or traditional email platforms."

Garrison had been doing one-on-one therapy with Vinessa for almost a year. He knew she had a mother who had died too soon and an overprotective father who doubled-down on Vivian's emotional wounds when he was murdered seven years later. Those deaths left Vinessa wounded for life and made Vince dangerous. He constantly hovered. That's why Vince was leery about therapy—he did not like anyone questioning him, or her.

Vince's body language gave off classic tells. His smugness came out in how he cocked his head to the side, always questioning everything. His scorn for luddites like Garrison was expressed as a quick, disgusted snort.

"Fifft. You ain't got an ounce of Geek in you, do you dude? You talk, talk, talk, but you never say shit about what's really top of the stack for anonymous people, do you? You think it's like privacy, don't you—it ain't! Privacy died last century. Guys like you are tracked on the Internet every second. Search engines, downloaders, hackers, scratchers, phishers, and sabs all over Russia and South Asia on your ass every second and you don't even know it. You search for something; they got you. You ask about herpes, they think you got it. You been bubbled for years and can't see it. You only got one IP address and that's plain stupid. Worst of all, you think you're private when you click some pathetic tab like 'private mode' or 'in-private browsing.' I'm right, ain't I?"

"Vince," Garrison said, trying to use a measured tone, "sometimes, when I'm doing focused research on a disturbing patient symptom, or a mental health diagnosis, I search and read private websites. All professional clinicians do."

"Shit you say. Those tabs are there to fool you, my man. All that happens is you disable cookies and make it hard for your computer to store websites. But those tabs grab hold of your IP address. And besides, your ISP knows what you're doing—where you're surfing—tabs or not. Shit, man, you might be a little private from smashing cookies, but you ain't effin' anonymous."

"All right, how do we make our family trust accounts anonymous?"

"You don't. I do that. That's why I'm here, dude. The first trick is to go somewhere in the cloud where your IP address, and your ISP can't see you."

"How is that possible?"

"Hey, it's not even that hard. You just have to make yourself dark, darker, as darkest you can by slithering through layers online, like you were on the bottom of the ocean. It's all dark down there. Some things live best in the dark. That's why it's called the Dark Web."

"Vince, humor me. I'm the novice you think I am. I don't know how to reach the Dark Web or store our documents there. We have to keep them safe from prying eyes, like the government. Each family will get two or three trust documents. Those documents provide creditor protection for the financial yield built into our family trust accounts. I can make pdfs of the docs, but I cannot find them if you put them in there, wherever *there* is. Can you do that *and* show me how to retrieve them when needed?"

"Well, my man, I already started that project—years ago before our dad was killed. I used VPNs to access and manipulate the new identity documents Vivian wanted back then—for us—and for the people she worked for. That's where the first family money came from—her work. I can show you where they are. It's easy if you know the passwords and logons. We own those VPNs. I mean, the family does. You sure Vinessa wants me to tell you all that stuff?"

Garrison could see doubt in Vince's eyes; he was conflicted. He understood, at least vaguely, that if she was here, he could not be. Pressing his lips together, he moistened them, slowly puffing his cheeks out, then inhaling. Vince showed him the digital track, click-by-click from a commercial browser, to a very different AI program, and from there using VPNs down into the Dark Web and over seventy family identity folders. It looked to him like a digital treasure chest opening to display financial opportunities like he'd never imagined. But that wasn't all Vince helped Garrison with.

"Yo, Garrison, lemme guess—you don't know shit about IP addresses, right?"

"Just that they are like street addresses for houses. My computer has one. I guess I've never worried about that."

"You're mostly right. See, the full name is *Internet Protocol Address*. Geeks shortcut to IP Address. It's like a government address of this house, only the house is your PC, get it?"

"So it identifies people who live in the house, or what?"

"No, not who lives here. Your computer's IP address allows messages to go out and come in via different apps, like email, or Instantashit, or freakin' Facebook. But hackers and other geeks see it as a bloody fingerprint for your PC. Gives a dude and others a hook to track your computer's ass down, and lay on some *malicious activity*. Know what I'm saying?"

"Does that mean outsiders can find you by tracking or getting your computer's IP address?"

"Garrison, I ain't got the time to educate you on computer science, but lemme just say this. If a dude knows your IP address, and he knows his shit, he can connect to your computer directly. It's complicated. There are tens of thousands of ports for every IP address, and if you know your shit you can bust in, steal a dude blind and pretend they are him."

"So how do we prevent that? I mean we can't risk financial data of the trust families that Emergence Incorporated will be responsible for. Can we? Have you got, like, protection from that?"

"Well, one way is to put their data on a NAS device."

"What's that?"

"To simplify it for you, it's a little black box with wires coming out, and it sits close by on your desk. Think about it this way. A refrigerator has a built-in freezer inside. But some people also have a freezer by itself, not connected to the refrigerator. So you got your beef steaks and a bottle of Vodka in the freezer part of your refrigerator, but you keep your frozen venison, a plastic bag of cash, and your bulk shrimp, cheese, and maybe a ham shank in the freezer, out in the garage. It's all about shelf life, my man. Freezing gives you longer shelf life than just keeping it cool in the refrigerator. Vinessa knows about shelf life—man, does she ever know about that."

"I didn't know she had a separate freezer."

"It's in the garage. But, see, a NAS device should be kept close by your computer because of your router. You know about routers, right?"

"I've heard the name, but that's about it. I know you need one if you're surfing the net."

"A router, my man, does your computer talking for you. It connects to the Internet. That's how it gets its name—it routes traffic between your devices and the Internet."

"But I can get to the Internet just with my laptop, like when I go to Starbucks."

"Yeah, on their dime. You're using Starbucks's Wi-Fi and their router. That router has an IP address. You use it. Bingo-jingo, you're surfing."

"So, Vince are you saying we need a NAS to protect us from hackers, or is it to help us access our files regarding the family trust agreements and the financial terms and accounts that back up those agreements?"

"I ain't saying one way or the other. But if you have a NAS device on a local network I'm saying those files and financial accounts would not have to be on some other dude's cloud server, like the freakin bank. Ya know the thing about a NAS device is that it doesn't have to call home. Know what I mean? It doesn't share the data with your computer unless you let it. You or Vinessa. You both are in the house where NAS is. Got it?"

"Well, now I got it. I guess I was thinking of it as backup. But now I see it as primary. Let me ask you this, could we back up the data on the NAS thing—the black box you're talking about—to a large capacity cell phone?"

"Yeah, you could do that, depending on storage capacity on the phone. Most NAS boxes have monster storage. But you could always use BitTorrent Labs. They have a robust momma bear with end-to-end encryption. Now, say you didn't trust those Apple biters. I don't. So, I'd back up the little black box to an Android phone. You can buy Android phones now with 528GB in storage, just don't fuck it up with stupid apps. They eat up storage like a hog in a corn bin."

Four hours later, after Vince's tutoring lesson and his four-mile hike up into North Mountain Park, Garrison changed clothes. Then, from the sitting room in the casita, he could see across the pool. Vinessa was in the main kitchen making lunch. He walked around the pool and knocked on the sliding door glass.

"Garrison, you're just in time. I'm making grilled cheese sandwiches for us. There's two bottles of Trader Joe's mineral water in the fridge. Would you get them for us? Let's eat out on the pool deck, OK?"

After lunch and small talk, he asked about the Emergence Incorporated documents that "someone" prepared before she became his patient in Australia.

"You mean the membership lists and identity documents for each family?"

"Yeah, those documents."

"Well, you know I didn't do them. The identity business, making up false names and new lives, was Vivian's way of getting us and Dad out of the stern eyes of the US Marshals office. We were in the US Federal Witness Protection Program. She had help; I remember that, with the Internet. What was it? It had a name, Tor or Thor, some Viking name, or maybe Greek. I know it was a secret place that you could not reach even with Internet Explorer. Now, of course, everything's Google Chrome."

Garrison tested her, saying, "OK, Vinessa, that helps. I've had other patients that used what is called the Dark Web. You access it by using software and a search engine called TOR. I think it's mostly used for marketplaces where illicit goods are bought and sold."

"Oh no. Vivian is so honest and everything. She'd never have us in a place where they did anything illicit. Are you talking about drugs, guns, or what?"

"Well, truthfully, one former patient of mine was a prisoner and had been released to a halfway house that gave me hourly work. She was in the stolen credit card business and used TOR to buy and sell the numbers off those cards."

"Well, I never. I mean Vivian did the work while I was traveling. She had help. I'm sure. But why are you asking about that now?"

"Because in our new venture, we'll be adding family trust relationships to the existing identity packages the company has sold for three years. To do that we will involve the same bank accounts, 401(k) plans, houses, and maybe other physical things they all have under the identities you or Vivian created for them."

"Of course you have my permission to work all that out with Vivian, or whoever else you want to consult with. I like your idea and am hopeful our people will like it too."

He hoped she got it. He didn't need to talk to Vivian— he needed Vince.

Garrison walked off the deck, out through the side gate, and then across the street to the footpath that led to the mountain preserve. He found a large, almost flat rock to sit on. A half hour later he walked back up the hill to the house and came back to his casita. He could hear music. It wasn't Vinessa. She hated rap.

"OK, Vince," he said over the whiney voice rhyming at max speed, "I got it cleared. Show me where and how to get new documents secured on TOR."

"Not so fast, doctor man. And while I'm at it, are you a real doctor?"

"I never said I was a doctor. I'm a nurse practitioner with special emphasis in mental health and addiction issues."

"Shit to me," Vince said. "Way I understand it is you're selling secret trust plans, whatever 'n shit that is, to Vinessa's multi-multi friends that we been gathering for three years now. Can you explain why they will give up their houses 'n shit, antique Corvettes, and 401 cays?"

"Vince, you and I are stuck with each other. You know that, right? Let's just work together but not get in each other's way in building this business. I'll create the documents we need to send to our Emergence Incorporated members. You create access to the Dark Web to secure all that data, especially the financial consequences. And you show me how to access it, like for times when you're not around. Can we work together to do that?"

"Bingo, my man. That's my super power. I know computers and the web. You know accounting and money. Vinessa has bought your plan. I'm here to push it off the cliff down to where no prying IRS eyes can see it. Deal?"

"Deal," Garrison said. *And no US Marshals or FBI either.*

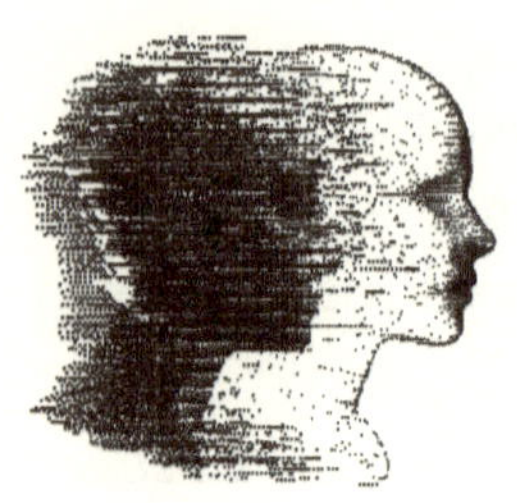# CHAPTER 9

One of the first things Garrison learned about the families who paid dues to Emergence Incorporated was how careful they were about names. He was conversant with the company files now that he'd gotten a detailed protocol from Vince that allowed him to access the files via TOR. Even so, he made a mistake on his first effort to entice an identity member to buy into the family trust protection plan. He knew the names in the files were their "new" names, the ones they all picked to replace their birth and married names. Their original names were also in the files, along with a smattering of details about where they came from and where they went with their new identities.

He picked a family at random to write the first email. He sent it to Lars Gustafson at LGninetythree@aol.com. Fifteen minutes later, he got a terse email.

"Who are you? What is the correct spelling of our last name?"

He took a second look at the actual file via TOR on the left side of his double monitor set-up. The mistake was right there. He'd spelled Gustafson the Americanized way—with one "f." The file confirmed the correct spelling—two f's. He replied, apologizing for not using two f's in the last name, and said he worked for Vivian and Vince. Within seconds, he got a second reply.

"OK, just checking. Are we still safe? Is Vivian still in charge?"

"Yes, Vivian is in charge but is out of time at the moment. Vinessa is assuming more responsibilities and has a new opportunity for you. I am her accountant and her therapist. May I send you another email with an encrypted file for your consideration? You won't need any software; once you open the file, it will be in plain text. Is that all right with you?"

Gustaffson's typed reply was exactly what Garrison hoped to hear.

"Yes, if it gives us more protection. More anonymity. Then we trust you. We are not at our old physical address anymore. We exist, for business purposes only on Tor."

"Well, Mr. Gustaffson, that is a wise decision on your part. I'll tell Vinessa as soon as she comes to the office, and . . ."

The email inbox went silent for a few moments, then dinged to announce another incoming. "Who is Vinessa?"

Garrison checked the email trail and realized the confusion.

"Sorry, Mr. Gustaffson, my error. Vivian is out of time, but Vinessa is here overseeing all member's files and the new family trust offering we are making to members. I'm sure you understand."

Two minutes later the reply appeared on his screen.

"Thanks. Yes, I understand. In fact, Lars is himself out of time and I'm here in his stead. I'm Lacy and will be happy to consider the family trust offering. When will we be getting documents to review?"

Pushing his breath out and shaking his fingers above the keyboard, Garrison answered, "In about ten days. Thank you ever so much. You will find the offering comforting and rewarding at the same time. In these troubled days of COVID-19 attacking our physical health, and the economy threating our financial health, all of us must look to new ways to stay alive and protect our financial assets."

CHAPTER 10

$\mathbb{G}$arrison's education as an accountant included courses covering the basics of tax and accounting issues in family trusts. But he had never studied trusts as legal solutions. Hoping that the trust document they had from Alberta Sundersen's law firm could be used as a form, he spent more hours re-reading it. It was obtuse and stunningly repetitive. He'd long been in the habit of using Microsoft Word tables to organize his thoughts. So he opened his computer and prepared a table. *Maybe,* he thought, *this will help me explain and write trusts for Emergence Incorporated people that they could understand.*

As Vince put it, "You need a dirt-plain document for people on the lam." He ended up with fifteen lines in a two-column table box.

Table Explaining Trust Terms in Non-lawyer Language for Emergence Incorporated Members

1. Grantor	Someone who creates the trust.
2. Trustee	Someone with the duty to manage the money in the trust.
3. Beneficiary	Someone who gets benefits from the trust.
4. Successor Trustee	Someone who takes over when the grantor dies or gets Alzheimer's.
5. Revocable	Something that can be struck off, changed, or voided.
6. Irrevocable	Not changeable, meaning the money stays where it is and the grantor can't take it back.
7. Living Trust	Something done when the grantor was still alive. Lawyers call it a testamentary trust.
8. Estate Taxes	Very complicated because these trusts give families the chance to receive estate tax savings for married people. Somehow it allows the beneficiary to keep family wealth available to a surviving spouse and children for things like health, support, maintenance, and education.
9. Income Distribution	When the grantors die, successor trustees take charge. They distribute money according to the beneficiaries' style of living and within trust assets.
10. COVID-19 Issues	If the grantor contracts a terminal illness or becomes irreversibly comatose then the doctors consult with successor trustees about pulling the plug.
11. Jointly Owned Property	This can be a problem if property is jointly held but not titled over to the trust.

12. Pour-over Wills	The marital trust has a provision that relates to the surviving spouse's will. It may dispose of the assets in the marital trust. If the surviving spouse has no will or the will has been revoked, the surviving spouse's marital portion would eventually "pour-over" to the family trust.
13. Double Death	The trust solves this. It says with simultaneous death that both spouses are deemed to have survived the other.
15. Surviving Spouse Access	He or she has general access to all money based on four conditional uses: health, support, maintenance, and education.
14. Trustee's Powers	Some trusts outlive their trustees if they are people. So banks, trust companies, or other corporate entities become trustees. Then it can replace dead family members. A corporate trustee can do anything that the grantor could have done.
15. Need for a Will	You need one even if you have a trust. Sometimes people who have trusts forget to title all their assets as trust assets. They make mistakes by titling assets in their own names. If the title is a deed, then the wording in the deed controls. If the deed is a joint tenancy, it automatically passes to the surviving spouse outside of the trust and not subject to the will. But when the second spouse dies, the joint tenancy property comes into the trust through the pour-over clause in the surviving spouse's will.

Garrison woke up the next morning to the smell of fried bacon wafting in from the kitchen. He knew Vinessa was back. He showered and put on a crisply starched white shirt with a maroon tie and walked around the pool deck to her kitchen door. With his new table list in hand, he said, "Good morning, Vinessa. Breakfast smells great. And I have lots to talk about."

"Well look at you, Garrison, wearing a starched shirt, and a tie. Not a pretty tie, I'd say, but one a lawyer might wear. Is that what you want to talk about, the legal stuff in your living trust plan for our members?"

"Ah, you guessed it just from the color of my tie, right?"

"Well, it's purple. It's a combination of red and blue. Someone once told me it was the color of the law but I can't remember why that's so. Do you know?"

"I do," Garrison said, as he cut his pancake into small squares with his fork. "Purple was the color worn by magistrates of the Roman Empire. Later on it became the imperial color worn by rulers and Roman Catholic bishops."

They small talked their way through breakfast. He said he'd do the dishes if she would give him a half hour out by the pool to talk about revocable family trusts and the future of Emergence Incorporated. She went to the master suite to change and he organized talking points in his head.

"So, Vinessa, I'm quite thrilled to tell you I've done all the legwork for drawing up family trust agreements and have written a draft for Lars and Valentina Gustaffson. I've talked to him and he's given the go-ahead to send him a draft. Do you remember him?"

"No, but Valentina Gustaffson wears the pants in that family. She was one of the first group of people who asked me to help them escape. I remember talking to her on the phone—she had a strong Italian accent but her husband was Finnish. Valentina suffers from DID. She's the dominant personality. I was never sure about him, except that he was agreeable. Didn't talk much, but she made up for it. And she looked at all the details carefully."

"Well, maybe that's still the case. I read the file documents, including their move from Maine to British Columbia and the work you did getting them settled in a new country, but at the same kind of jobs."

"I'm just saying, Garrison, that you should talk to her too. But go ahead; tell me how this would work for that family."

"Okay, I made a copy of the draft agreement for you. Let's go through it paragraph by paragraph. The title is there on top and most of the first page is just for naming it as a revocable trust agreement. Then, it says there, Lars N. Gustaffson and Valentina G. Gustaffson, grantors, declare they have transferred and delivered to the trustee all their joint and separate interests in the property described in Schedule A, attached to this Declaration of Trust. The trustee hereby acknowledges receipt of the trust property and agrees to hold the trust property in trust, according to this Declaration of Trust."

"Garrison, what property are they transferring?"

"I don't know. This is the draft I'll upload to them via the TOR channel Vince created for this project. They will go through the document to make sure it's what they want and they will fill out Schedule A. Once that's done, and they sign the trust agreement, we will move to the next phase."

"Is it a permanent transfer? What if they change their minds?"

"That's covered in Part Four. You can see that there on page three. It says, 'The grantor may amend or revoke this trust at any time, without notifying any beneficiary. An amendment must be made in writing and signed by the grantor. Revocation may be in writing or any manner allowed by law.'"

"That's confusing," Vinessa said. "Is amending the same thing as revoking?"

"No, not the same. They can make any amendments they want at any time. We just change the agreement and they sign it again. Revocation is different. If they revoke the agreement, then the property they put in trust comes out and goes back to whatever form they want."

"Well, that's good. Most of our people have moved more than once and a few have changed their identity several times. I think if very many of our members do this trust thing, you will be busy making changes. What's next?"

"Take a look at Part Five there on page four. It's titled, 'Payments from Trust During Grantor's Lifetime.' As you can see, this says that 'the trustee shall pay to or use for the benefit of the grantor as much of the net income and principal of the trust property as the grantor requests. Income shall be paid to the grantor at least annually. Income accruing in or paid to trust accounts shall be deemed to have been paid to the grantor.' This is really the engine in the agreement. This is where the Mr. and Mrs. Gustaffson will make money on their money, but in private, and invisible to the world."

"But isn't the grantor also the trustee? I think that's what you told me last week when we talked."

"Yes and no. In many family trusts, the mother and father are both the grantors and the trustees of their own trust. But remember, our members are living under new identities, in secret places. They are in hiding and won't want to be trustees. They will be grantors, but Emergence Incorporated will be the trustee for them."

"Can a corporation be a trustee?"

"Sure, a trustee can be an individual, two or more individuals, or a business entity such as a corporation. A business entity serving as trustee is typically a bank, law firm, or other professional trustee company."

"But our corporation, Emergence Inc., isn't a bank or a law firm. I remember you telling me that corporations are legal fictions. They exist only to serve their owners."

"Yes, that's right," Garrison said, feeling a twinge of hesitation on Vinessa's part. He'd seen this in her several times. She'd draw her brows closer together and thumb her ear.

"How in the world could I be a trustee? I can handle my own financial affairs, with help from you when it comes tax time, but I don't know much about investing or safeguarding other people's money."

"Well, that's why I'm setting it up this way. The trustee on these trusts will be Emergence Inc. your corporation. It will be the named trustee in all the trusts. It can then hire investment advisors, financial experts, maybe tax accountants to create suitable investment opportunities. Remember our idea that we could almost promise them three percent per annum on their money? That is paid by banks or mutual funds. We pick the banks and the funds and report most of the income in their accounts to them, except for our fee for managing the money for them. They will love this because they know you and appreciate all you've already done for them. This is just more help you're offering to keep them prosperous and their money and assets away from prying eyes."

"Who would pick the mutual funds or bonds or whatever? You?"

"Well, yes. I guess it has to be me at the start. I know quite a bit about investing my own money and have always given advice to patients who asked me for that, along with therapy. I see this as a way for everyone to make money—the members, you, your company, and me."

"Garrison, I hate to bring it up again, but that's not why we started this company. We did it because most of our first members were in the federal government's Witness Protection Program. And they hated all that watching and interfering. Now, won't our members say we are watching and interfering with their money?"

"No they won't and here's why. They don't know how to invest because they've been in hiding and want to stay that way. I know how to find the right places to invest their excess cash. They won't be putting in money they need to live on, just money they have that is uninvested, not drawing interest, or dividends. And lastly, many of them won't put cash in the trust. They will put real property, like homes, or personal property like cars, or maybe even artwork. That's a way to get tax benefits and secure homes for long periods of time after the first spouse dies."

"Does it say that in the trust agreement?" Vinessa asked.

"Yes, well at least partly. Further on, the agreement defines the word 'Revocable' as it relates to how long the trust lasts. It's a revocable trust, and the income earned by the trust is reported on the grantor's individual tax return, Form 1040. As far as income taxes are concerned, the IRS doesn't recognize the existence of a revocable trust. There is no need to file a separate tax return until after the death of the grantor. One of the articles in the agreement provides for the distribution of all income and principal to the grantor during life."

"So the trustee, my company, is sort of like the family bookkeeper—is that a good analogy?

"No, ma'am, not at all. The trustee is much more than a bookkeeper. A better analogy would be multiplicity itself. The trustee is really an altar of the dominant personality. Look at Section B, the 'Specified Powers of Trustees.' It's a long list of what the trustee does for the grantors."

Vinessa turned to page 7 and read aloud. "Trustee has the power to hold property in trust, sell trust property, borrow money, encumber trust property, manage trust real estate as if the trustee were the absolute owner of it, make repairs or alterations, insure against loss, buy and sell stocks, bonds, debentures, and any other form of security or security account, at public or private sale for cash or on credit, including buying on margin."

"My goodness, Garrison, this gives the trustee a lot of power. Do the Gustaffson's really understand this? I'd say the trustee is more an alter ego of the grantor than merely an alter of a different personality state. You know alters are transient. Temporary. They have no real power, at least not like this."

"You're right. But in living trusts, the important part is how well the property is managed and how long the protection against estate taxes lasts. And there's more you didn't read. If your members elect to create these living trusts, Emergence Incorporated can make a real difference in their lives, and the lives of their offspring. It can receive new property at any time without more documentation. To make sure everything is kosher it can retain experts like CPAs and trust and estate lawyers. It actually holds the funds the grantors put into the trust. It can buy, sell, margin, move money, and enter into electronic fund transfer or safe deposit arrangements with financial institutions."

"But Garrison, that comes back to trust and confidence. I just can't see giving an outsider that kind of power. I never would do that, and I started this whole business—well, not actually. Vivian started it while she was out of time."

"Vinessa," Garrison said, leaning forward across the coffee table. "You are underestimating the trust your people have in you. They are living well because of you. They have businesses you helped them build. This trust agreement goes to the heart of that relationship. If you kept reading you'd get down to the part that says the trustee has the power to continue any business of the grantor. It means even after the death of the grantor, and in some cases after the death of the second spouse. At that point, the trust becomes irrevocable. It may not be amended or altered except as provided in the agreement. Of course, the trustee has to pay the grantor's debts, estate taxes, and expenses of the grantor's last illness and funeral. But if there are minor children or grandchildren, the trust continues until they reach the age of majority."

Garrison watched Vinessa sink back into the cushions of her chair. He had walked her carefully through months of therapy after the capture and supposed death of Julia Santerra-Evans in Texas three years ago. He knew she, beyond all expectations, was a confirmed optimist, always looking for the bright side. She felt so much loyalty to her members, her *people* as she called them. He'd marveled at how often he heard her singing love songs and ballads in perfect pitch, but always when she was alone. By helping others to hide from their reality, she found healing of her own emotional wounds. Since she had no genetic family of her own, she hung on to her members as if they were family, even sending them private and unsigned cards on Valentine's Day. The family trust discussion had her on the verge of tears and joy simultaneously.

Dabbing her eyes with Kleenex, she said in a voice so low he had to lean forward. "Garrison, this is so wonderful that it scares me."

"Scares you?"

"Yes, we can help them so much, it seems like a dream. But my dreams rarely came true. If you are absolutely sure we can do this safely, without risking their anonymity or money, then we should start right away."

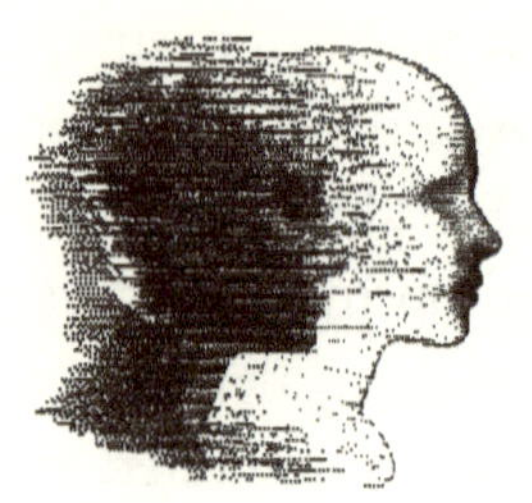

CHAPTER 11

It took less than an hour to finalize the Gustaffson draft trust agreement. Garrison uploaded it to their encrypted VPN on the TOR channel Vince created. He attached it to the electronic messaging system embedded in the account. His email, based on the single short exchange with Lars, was as short as he could make it.

> Mr. and Mrs. Gustaffson, Vivian and Vinessa asked me to send the attachment to you for your consideration. She thinks it will help you as you proceed with a life lived in quiet but unknown spaces, as she is doing herself. I do not make decisions on these family trust agreements. I only communicate your wishes to her. Please reply at your convenience as to whether you are interested in creating a trust for your extended family. If you

wish, you can call me at the number listed below with questions or concerns. She wishes you well.

He hit send and decided to take a swim. While changing his t-shirt and Levis for a swimsuit in the casita bathroom, he heard the familiar bell tone on his computer. He crossed the room and saw the typed message thread—*To Emergence Incorporated.*

This is Valentina. I make decisions on our end. We like proposal. We like that our Vivian is doing so well she can help us another time. We have tax person here but knows only Canadian law. We want to get more money to help one child and two adults who no longer live with us. It will take one hour to get notarized signatures, but more hours to list the properties we now own. Vivian might remember living in trailer park in Idaho. We own seven like the one she told me about—five in Canada, one in Idaho, one in Washington State. Do we need copies of titles to deeded property, and survey plats to send to you? How about values of our properties? We can say what we pay, but who knows value today? What happens if we sell one after we title it over to Emergence, Inc, the said trustee in your form? Send reply your soonest. Valentina.

He printed the reply and read it quickly, then slowly, and then a third time, underlining in red the questions Mrs.

Gustaffson asked. Shaking his head from side to side and smiling like a crescent moon, he typed his answer.

Mrs. Gustaffson. Vinessa is very happy you want to let us help you and your family. Your trailer park properties are good examples of properties you can add to your trust. We need the complete legal description from the county recorders where the parks are located. When you send those, we will create new deeds confirming that you are deeding over to Emergence Incorporated those properties to be held in trust for your family. Those deeds will be sent back to you for notarized signatures. We will make the necessary filings in Arizona, where your trust will be legally established. Give us your best estimate of value—no need to get a formal appraisal, but you can if it is convenient for you. Once you title a property over to Emergence Inc. as your trustee, you cannot sell it. But you own the trust, so you can direct us, as your trustee, to honor any sale you have agreed to make. The title can be reverted to you because the trust is revocable. The terms and conditions regarding this are explained in Parts 1, 3, 4, and 5 of the trust agreement. One more thing, do you have cash assets or stock positions that you want to add to your trust? They will give you a return of at least three percent per annum, minus our modest fees for handling. If the bank where you have money is paying more than that, good for you. Just keep it

there. Thank you for trusting Vivian and Vinessa.
They value your friendship.

He hit send and leaned back in his chair, hands cradling his neck, letting this first success rebound back and forth from his monitor. He halfway envisioned another rocket reply, but nothing came, so he went to the pool.

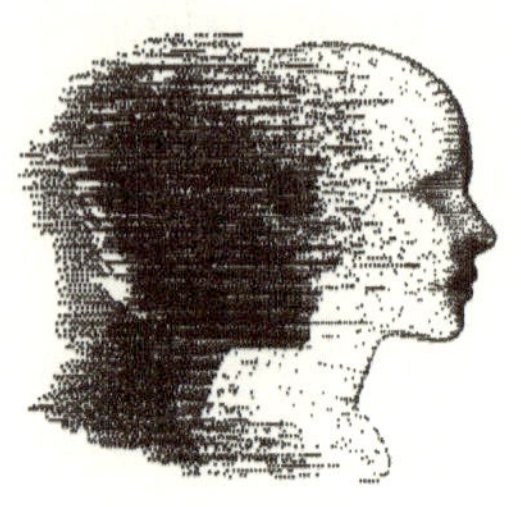

CHAPTER 12

He didn't see Vinessa the next morning. The kitchen glass wall was dark until almost noon when he noticed her across the pool, at the sink. She was wearing a robe and a shower cap. Rather than walk across, he thought it best to text her. "Afternoon, boss. Got some time for me this afternoon? Therapy session?"

He saw her reach into the pocket of her robe and fish her iPhone out. As she read the text, she turned around to face the pool area and waved at him.

His text tone sounded and he tabbed it on. "I see you Garrison. Yes. We should. Four o'clock—teatime? In the living room?"

Texting back with a smiley face, he typed, "Got It," and waved at her. She disappeared back into the interior of the house. At 4 p.m. on the dot, he walked through the side gate to the front yard and knocked on the front door screen.

"Right on time, Garrison," she said. "It's unlocked. Come in, please."

She had set a tray on the coffee table between the two leather couches. Tea, with a miniature milk pour, real sugar in a bowl, and matching china cups and saucers. As he sat down, she said, "You're looking too thin, Garrison. Take two spoonfuls of this wonderful cane sugar."

He told her the family trust project was coming along and that he'd identified thirty-six members who might be interested.

"How did you select them? We don't know anything about their financial status, do we?"

"Well, actually we do. Not much, but enough to guess some need on their part. All thirty-six people on this list live in zip codes that *The Washington Post* says are 'Super Zips.'"

"Whatever are Super Zips?" she asked, swirling a half-teaspoon of milk into her teacup.

"A financial analysist with a penchant for statistics wrote a column. It seems like artificial intelligence computers can organize around average family income and college degrees. Then you can search with those two in a Boolean-style search with the word 'zip code' in the string. The result of that search are Super Zips, chock full of high-income and high educational attainment. They are mostly located in New York and the DC metro area. But they also exist in San Jose, Oakland, Newark, and Los Angeles. Paradise Valley, Arizona, is one and you have an Emergence Incorporated family living there."

"Really? Paradise Valley? That's just a few miles from here. That makes me nervous. Don't send your flyer to them—too close—too close."

"Vinessa, that's a surprise. What difference would that make? We won't be in physical contact with any member who wants a family trust. It's all done in the Dark Web."

"Well, what about banks? And insurance? And brokerage houses? You are planning on placing members' money in local banks or trust companies, aren't you? Wouldn't that require an occasional personal visit? Maybe to a safe deposit box for bearer bonds or the like?"

"No, I was not thinking of anything like that. I've been identifying offshore trust banks that only do business online. And some cyber investments as well. They all pay more than three percent and that's where we will make some money and secure fees."

"Garrison, you're scaring me again. I know we've talked about security and safety. We cannot take risks. I've been reading about facial recognition systems and how prevalent they are, especially in banks. So, I like your idea about online banking arrangements, but I'm not at all confident with this offshore idea."

"Vinessa, please hear me out. You lived in London and Sydney and did business with offshore entities from time to time. Most of it is legitimate business. The shady drug stuff is mostly done in Panama and other Central American locales. We'll avoid that. I'm thinking Europe and Australia as offshore. But please, let me change the subject, if you don't mind."

"Change the subject?" she asked pensively.

"Yes, remember my text this morning? I said we needed a therapy session this afternoon. I have something we need to talk about."

"Oh, so you did. We missed last week, didn't we?"

"Yes, and the week before last as well. We could switch to once a month because you're doing so well, but there is one thing we should talk about today. It's about names and mottos."

She sat very still for a minute. Looking at him, then down, then back at him, like he was fading in and out of her vision. Rubbing her forehead with her fingertips, she kept silent. He dared not interrupt her apparent need to think in front of him. Finally, she nodded in his direction.

"Names and mottos? That's Freudian isn't it? He was the first to examine people's unconscious thoughts, feelings, and memories. Right? Names are entangled thoughts and mottos are expressions of deeper needs, aren't they? Is that where you're going?"

"No, not at all. Freudian psychoanalysis is a disputed clinical tool. At best it's marginalized because both the academic and clinical communities have abandoned it. What we should talk about therapeutically are your names and your mottos. We've talked around those issues, now we need to take them head on. You are Vivian; you know that, right? Yes, you were correctly diagnosed with a dissociative identity disorder, but your alter is Vince, right? Not Vinessa. Vinessa is a name you've selected for yourself now that you are a little older, no longer as threatened, or as vulnerable. But Vinessa is a nickname, an alias, a *nom de plume*, right? It's how you express yourself today. You're Vivian with a new name, right?"

"Yes. I'm still Vivian. I've outgrown the pigtails, no longer wear cowboy boots, and I'm definitely not a tomboy. I look different. I feel different. I'm an older her, with much better makeup. Back then, in the pigtail days, I had to be somebody else. I grew up knowing what happened, but not why. Vince was not me, I thought. He's himself. But over time I realized he was me, and he saved me many times. I was suicidal and then it went away because he was not. I hated my life but he loved his. Now, with help from you and Dr. Estancia in Houston, and lots of clinical reading, I know what I know. The experts say DID patients do not know their alters and cannot remember things that happen when time stops or starts again. I'm sure that's true for others, but I do remember many things. Maybe not everything, but in time I can bring it back and see Vince in my mind. I don't recognize him, but he's there in my memory."

"Vinessa, that's good to hear. I've tried to broach the subject before but decided you were not ready. Now, can we talk about mottos?"

"Sure, but I don't have one, do I?"

"Yes, you do. I mentioned it just yesterday when we were talking about the family trust project. Your motto has been for years, 'You Are Who You Say You Are.' Remember that?"

"Okay, sure. That's a motto from way back, when I didn't have a *nome de plume*. I told Dad and Vince that. I got it out of a book I borrowed from the Cranston Library. It's a mind over matter thing. We ducked out of the US Marshal's Witness Protection Program, made up new names, and used our new names with the new people we met after we scrammed out of Arizona. We became the people we said we were and no one doubted it. It's really amazing when you think about it. You could go to college as a freshman, pick a new first name, and it would stick no matter what your grade sheet said or your diploma. You became exactly whoever you said you were. Why are we even talking about this now?"

"Because, both clinically and from a business perspective, now you have to be whoever you *think* you are."

"Sorry, Garrison. I don't get it. What's thinking got to do with it?"

"Here's a good example. When you moved from Vivian to Vinessa, it was because you were older and wanted a different persona to present to people you came into contact with, like Dr. Estancia and me. But there was no reason you had to think you were a different person. Now there is. Vivian and Vinessa are the same person, but only Vinessa can change the way she thinks. Vinessa is the owner and chief executive of a business that might become a conglomerate. You're no longer just in the business of helping people start new lives. You're now in the business of making a fortune by helping those same people protect their assets and avoid going to probate court years from now, when they die."

"A fortune? Garrison, I know you're excited about this stuff, but a fortune? Really? We will make money by charging fees, but even if all thirty-six or even more families sign up, it's still their money, not ours."

"No, Vinessa. The potential is much higher than you think. That's why I hope you can embrace this new motto.

You are Who You Think You Are. That's thinking big. Thinking conglomerate. Think about this. Let's say the Gustaffson family has $100,000 they assign over to you, the trustee of their family trust. You've offered them three percent per annum. That's $3,000 per year. You pay them what you promised and they are happy. But the core one hundred grand is in your name and you have full authority to invest it any way you see fit. Let's say you find an investment that pays 10 percent per annum. That's $10,000. You credit their account for three thousand and invest the other seven thousand in a different account. That account returns ten percent to you, seven thousand dollars. So you now have $7,700 in that account. Take it one more step. Now let's say that account is average among the thirty-six accounts. Collectively you have $7,700 times thirty-six, which turns into $277,200 in one year. At compounding rates that will be well over two million dollars in just seven years. And that's just a start."

Vinessa went quiet. The smile evaporated. She started clicking her teeth together and twisting the napkin in her lap. Sensing something wrong, Garrison kept talking.

"Here's a glimpse of what the future could bring to Emergence Incorporated. What if our program grows real legs and we find a hundred families, not just thirty-six? The profit margin is nearly 100 percent, because it's in our control for years and years. You will be a multi-millionaire before you're forty. But to get there, you have to be 'who you *think* you are.' A businesswoman with a million-dollar idea. With these family trusts you can leave behind old wounds and old habits—your future is rich and waiting for you."

He got a reaction he had not remotely considered. She got mad. Red-in-the-face mad. Almost as quickly as she glared at him, she seemed to shrink within herself. The color drained from her face. Waving her hand to him, as though declaring a foul at a soccer match, she silenced him.

"Garrison, what are you trying to do to me? Don't you know what you're saying? Goddamn it. Goddamn everything. I never wanted to face the world after what the world did to me. My future is rich? That's what you just said. Rich! What about the lake, and the little boy who drowned because of me? I was only nine. Now you say all that is over—I'm going to be rich? Rich means famous. Rich means facing myself! Get out. Get out right now!"

Garrison didn't just walk out the front door; he scuttled out like a petulant teenager whose dad would not let him smoke in the house. Once back inside the casita, he closed the window shades and locked the door. It was that act, actually locking the door, that brought home what had just happened. He dug his medicine kit from under the sink in the bathroom. He'd had it for years—an old canvas pack with a tattered red cross emblem on the front. From a tin box, he picked one of the outdated Xanax pills and popped it in his mouth without the benefit of a swallow of water. It went down, but with some difficulty.

Vigorously rubbing his temples with his forefingers, he flopped down on the couch in the sitting room waiting for the first calming effects of the drug to kick in. In his clinical practice, he often recommended patients go to their family doctors and get a prescription for benzodiazepines.

He only did that when the natural relief of exercise, yoga, or tai chi didn't help. His mentor in graduate school had persuaded him to start with organic stress reduction first and move to drugs only when meditation didn't work. Deep down, he knew his stomach and his mind were telling him to do both. He mellowed into a half-sleep, half-awake doze. In less than a half hour, he was back physiologically, with his heart rate back down to the seventies and his oxygen saturation rate back up to the mid-nineties.

After making a pot of tea and drinking a large glass of water, he turned to the tool that worked best for him in these rare situations where a patient's clinical status became his own reality—he wrote clinical notes on what had just happened with Vinessa. On reflection, he knew she'd had a panic attack. But for the first time in his life, observing a patient's panic attack in real time had given him one.

Pt status–panic attack–iteration–realization
and recall of trauma–other child death–
age nine–renewal of guilt–likely overreaction
by parent—?–but no inner withdrawal into
alter state–?–why not?–assessment–is
this a transference reaction—?–Vinessa
or Vivian or Vince??–who is transference
agent–possibilities are alters–maybe me as
clinician–fear of losing control to who??–me?
or Vince!

He knew just by reducing the real life event to writing that the status quo was unacceptable to her, or him. It would take time to unravel and perhaps an upgrade in clinical care. Should he refer Vinessa to a psychiatrist? Who? Why? The thought made him a dizzy but he knew better than to take a meclizine tablet. Particularly on top of the Xanax. What other possibilities were there?

He went back to the bedroom and found the large leather brief bag he used to carry clinical reference papers. He fished out one with a chapter on countertransference. It had a short section on what he was thinking might explain Vinessa's meltdown and her anger with him. The short note said: "Classically, countertransference describes the clinician's emotions toward a client, typically unconscious in nature, and often a result of displaced emotions, stemming from the clinician's previous life experience, and having a detrimental effect on the relationship between clinician and client."

Is that what happened? he wondered. Dislike is a death knell in both directions. If you dislike your patient, or she dislikes you, it leads to a drastic negative impact on patient-clinician rapport. Usually, it ends up with an intervention. His lack of awareness was a pain in the side for him. He didn't see her reaction coming. Now mulling it over in his mind, stretching his memory for clues, he could not fathom how he missed it. *We both had good coping skills,* he thought, *but even so we're now in a countertransference framework. She doesn't understand me and I don't trust her.*

He spent a sleepless night and a slow early morning nursing a headache with black coffee and aspirin. He could see no movement on the other side of the pool. No lights, no upraising of the shades on the inside of the floor to ceiling glass walls. He was shaky about calling or texting, but Vinessa had always been good with email. On the subject line, he typed, Sorry, Vinessa, Can We Talk? In the body of the message, he tried to strike a neutral but purposeful tone.

> I know you're angry and that is on me. I was too familiar, not clinically objective, and at least a little bit out of order. We have much to think about and even more to do with the Family Trust Program in its infancy. Should I move out, rent something nearby, and meet with you by Zoom? Please know I'm very sorry and that I know you're hurt.

He didn't include a salutation, or a closing, but he did click on the TAGS tab to require a delivery receipt before hitting SEND.

Within seconds his ISP sent a delivery receipt noting that delivery was complete. Just a few minutes later, she wrote back. For her salutation, she wrote his first initial, G, and for her closing she wrote V. That said volumes about their relationship. The content was kinder, slightly forgiving, and contained good news.

> G
>
> You're not entirely to blame. We are who we are and you've helped to restore my confidence about my condition. You are who you are and that alone explains why we must now change our relationship.

I WILL NO LONGER BE YOUR PATIENT. BUT I VERY MUCH HOPE YOU WILL CONTINUE TO BE THE COMPTROLLER FOR EMERGENCE INC. THE COMPANY NEEDS YOU NOW MORE THAN EVER. MY MISTAKE WAS IN MIXING COMPANY BUSINESS, INDEED ITS FUTURE, WITH MY PERSONAL CLINICAL NEEDS AND FUTURE. IF YOU WILL STAY ON AS FINANCIAL MANAGER OF THE FAMILY TRUST BUSINESS, I WILL BE HAPPY AND WILL ALLOW YOU ALL THE LATITUDE YOU NEED TO MAKE THE VENTURE SUCCESSFUL. I HAVE MORE TO SAY ON THIS IF YOU ARE WILLING TO CONTINUE. WE WILL NOT MEET IN PERSON EVER. I WILL BE OUT OF ARIZONA BY TOMORROW. DO NOT TRY TO FIND ME. WE CAN DISCUSS DETAILS TOMORROW. IF YOU WANT TO COMPLETELY BOW OUT, JUST SAY SO NOW.

V

His reply was short but he hoped that it mirrored her tone.

V

OF COURSE I WANT TO STAY ON AS YOUR COMPTROLLER. I BELIEVE THE FAMILY TRUST BUSINESS WILL BE ENORMOUSLY SUCCESSFUL AND AM EAGER TO DISCUSS ITS FUTURE AND MY TERMS. I KNOW YOU'RE RIGHT ABOUT THERAPY. I WISH YOU THE BEST IN FINDING A SUITABLE CLINICIAN.

G

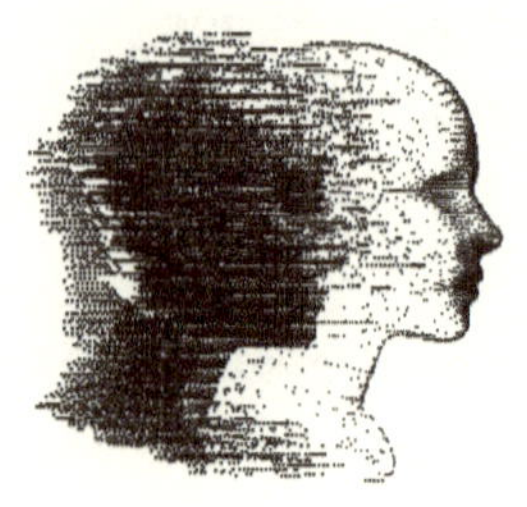# CHAPTER 13

Garrison tried to send Vinessa a text at 8:00 a.m. sharp the next morning but discovered her cell phone was "unavailable." He tried calling her but got a message that the number called was out of service. He called her telecommunications provider, pretended he was her brother, and learned she had quit AT&T. He tried her regular email address but got a response from his Outlook Exchange server: "Outlook Exchange does not recognize V@nuid .net." He tried to reply to yesterday's message but learned the recipient has discontinued this service. At 11:00 a.m., he heard an odd buzzing sound coming from his laptop. He opened to lid to see a grey screen with a small script message. "You have a new VOIP call. To answer this call please turn on your microphone."

He turned it on, put his headset on, and heard what sounded like a river running through a canyon with echoes. Then in seconds, she said, "Garrison, it's me."

"Vinessa, I was getting worried. I tried calling and . . ."

She interrupted saying, "Yes, well, I've changed my contacts lists. I'll give you a number when we finish this call. It will be good for one day at a time, and reroute automatically once you've entered a valid logon and password. Vince set this up and you know how complicated he can get. How are you this morning? Feeling better, I hope."

"Fine, thank you very much. You're not in Phoenix, I take it."

"That's the first thing we should talk about, Garrison. I have decided to disappear again. You won't know where I am. I may be absent at times because my VOIP numbers will change often. VOIP can be difficult in areas where broadband is inconsistent and time zones overlap. You can probably guess I'm no longer in the same country you are. That's best for both us—you know why, don't you?"

"No, Vinessa, I can't say that I do, but as long as you feel safe, I'm fine with it."

"It's not my safety that I'm thinking about. It's yours. Vince is not happy with our therapy session yesterday and you know he has a temper and a foul mouth. Suffice it to say we're oceans apart. I have some conditions, well, we all do, you know. Let's start there, OK?"

"Conditions about what?" he said, trying to steady his voice.

"Conditions about continuing to develop the family trust business. I've talked to my other financial advisor, a man you do not know. He's in Zurich. He knows only that I'm considering advancing some funds from my account there to fund a new business in the United States. The first condition really comes from him; he's a very conservative man when it comes to fiscal security. I will fund the family trust business by wire transfer to any offshore bank where you open an account. I do not want to risk Emergence Inc. funds for this new business. You tell me how much money you need to get the program started, including your salary and operating expenses for the first six months. We will refund every six months as needed so that the business is not run 'just for profit,' but solely to ensure the security of the trust assets. That's how he says I should do this."

"Well, V, if it's just operational funding, I'd say that's a fine idea. But the relationship between Emergence Inc. and individual members must stay the same as it is now. Remember that this whole operation depends entirely on the members' reliance on, and trust in, *you*. You name has to be on all the trust documents, as the CEO of Emergence Inc."

"Yes, I know that, and he assumes that will be the motivating factor to ensure enough volume to make the effort sustainable. That's how he thinks—financial efforts that are sustainable over ten-year blocks of time. He thinks family trusts will expand as long as the US Congress is in conservative control—they do protect the rich—that's what *America First* means, at least in the financial centers of Europe. But let's not go on with that. Tell me what your salary requirements will be."

"Honestly, V, I haven't given it any thought. But it ought to be compartmentalized, you know, a base salary for effort, and a bonus for results."

"Garrison, I do like it that you're calling me V rather than my chosen adult name. I'm talking for us—that is, the three of us. You scared Vivian and enraged Vince at the house, so now you're talking to me not as Vinessa but as the personality state I am. That's reassuring to them. Now back to business; shall I just wire, say, fifty thousand US dollars for operations? Will that be enough to engage at the operational level?"

"Yes, I suppose that's so. I can advise you as we move forward, and . . ."

"No, Garrison, that's another thing we must settle now. I do not want status reports or financial results. That data must be reported directly to the members, by you. They should be informed on a quarterly basis of financial results on their trust assets. But we do not want to know that information. We have to be outside the day-to-day; do you know what I mean?"

"With one major alteration, and that is that I conduct the business. And everything must be in your name. The members trust you, not me. I'll sign the financial reports. They will be pdfs attached to each member family on a quarterly basis. But for my own protection, I will want to use a *nome de plume* to protect my identity from them, just as the company has done to protect them from the government's peering eyes here. Is that OK with you?"

"Well, we will think that over. Now, what do you think about salary and bonus money? I can pay beginning and ongoing operational costs for all of your expenses, but the bonus money has to come from results over the basic 3-percent return paid to members. What is your thinking on that?"

Garrison leaned back on the swivel chair for a long moment. Then he had an idea.

"V, this is a startup. You're an angel investor and should recoup your investment in the operation of the trust business. But beyond that, I'm really the CEO on the financial side. I think I should be paid a salary consistent with what small bank CEOs are paid annually. I'd say two hundred fifty thousand per year, and . . ."

She interrupted, "Garrison, you're not a small bank CEO; you're a nurse practitioner with a degree in finance. I'll pay you seven thousand a month to run the family trust business and keep the accounts straight in the Dark Web, where Vince already has you set up. That should be enough. You can stay in the house, not just the casita, for the rest of the lease term. Do you accept that?"

This is the thanks I get, he thought, as he struggled for an answer. If he readily accepted, he'd look weak. But if he didn't, she might hang up, again. For the first time in a long time, Garrison felt a twinge of payback. She couldn't see him widening his eyes, blinking furiously, and reaching for a Kleenex, but she might have heard the intake of breath before he answered.

"Well, I suppose you're right. I do have to prove myself to you at a business level. And you were right to terminate our clinical relationship. So, I accept. The lease term is twelve months, but there's an option to renew at an 8.5-percent increase in monthly payments. This project may take longer than twelve months to develop. May I stay in the main house for as long as it takes, renewing the lease at least once?"

"I see no problem with that," she said quickly.

He didn't expressly agree with the seven grand salary, but by implication they both understood that was what he'd be paid.

"Fine," he said. "I won't trouble you with financial data but I'll let you know how many families sign up on a monthly basis, all right?"

"By text," she said.

He didn't say anything, wondering whether she'd just hang up, like before. He guessed right. He couldn't hear it, but he waited thirty seconds and then said hello. There wasn't even an echo. It was that event-ending conversation that triggered a smoldering memory from his own childhood. He realized the VOIP line was dead.

Emergence Inc. does not have shares and cannot bonus me with stock options, he realized. *It cannot compensate me in the public eye with tax-saving clauses. Stupid woman. Can't she get it? Given the novelty of this business, she should pay me 25 percent of the override.*

He used the calculator on his iPhone to convince himself. As he often did, he talked aloud to his phone when making calculations on the screen. "Assume fifty members set up plans and deposit $20,000 each. That's a million bucks. Emergence Incorporated gives them, collectively, three percent of one million dollars. That's thirty thousand dollars, leaving nine-hundred seventy thousand dollars in the collective account. A fair compensation bonus for producing that would be twenty-five percent, or $242,500. The 75-percent balance would stay in the account. Or maybe I should get back at her BIG TIME! Take it all! Fuck. Fuck!

She's probably going to terminate me once the business is up and running."

He was sweating in an air-conditioned casita. As he clicked in numbers and read results, he felt a palsy between his legs and a searing headache coming on.

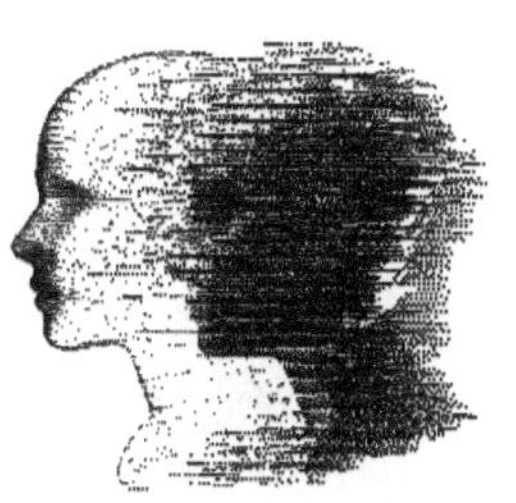

CHAPTER 14

When she hung up, just getting away from Vinessa's whine and weep felt good to him. At least, he thought, her voice on this call was her own. She was the one who had outed him. She probably listened to herself, that is, Vivian. *This is her doing, not Vince's,* he thought. As he mulled that over, he realized he might have more in common with Vince the alter than he had with Vivian/Vinessa the dominant personality state.

Now that Garrison was terminated as her therapist he felt no loss, and now that he'd been promoted from a mere comptroller to an executive position, without a title, he felt a deep-seated need to get even. *How dare they* echoed at him from his frontal lobe down to his gut. One was booming, the other growling. *How can I take advantage?* he thought, tapping the eraser-tipped pencil on the desktop. Turning to his notepad, he wrote his feelings, not hers, for the first time in almost two years.

Them—sneaking around my back—Me changing for the better—V is def passive aggressive—me—calculating and out in front—They want to avoid detection—Me ?? —That's right—me too—avoid detection at all costs—Them—disappeared years ago—Me disappear?—Damn straight—me too—but rich, for life—somewhere else—a country where being rich matters and identity doesn't—a ring of invisibility—perfect protection from the law, the families, and most of all—from the three V's.

Garrison's education was problematic. He'd spent two formative years at a community college developing modest social skills and a research perspective. Three more years at a state university brought financial knowledge and a sense that one man's financial success often came on the backs of failures by lesser-educated and more devious people. He earned a BSBA. Then, at grad school, he managed to put off the financial need to get rich while sharpening the need to understand psychology for himself, and others. Vinessa, Vivian, and Vince had stoked an unrequited need to strike back, get even, and get out.

And then, as he sat there morbidly recalling a past he'd buried, his brother settled in his brain. His twin. Who, like his parents, used him. Gilbert was him—in looks—but not in temperament. Gilbert was reclusive. Garrison was outgoing. Gilbert accepted God, in his fictional role as Jesus Christ, the savior. Garrison was an accident, but he knew no God and wrote his own book of commandments and sins. Quickly, Garrison shook off thinking about Gilbert. He always did what needed doing when thoughts of Gilbert overpowered him. He moved from the chair to the floor. Sat with his knees bent, feet flat, and arms encircling his legs. Then he rocked back and forth, biting down on his tongue, clicking his teeth, and crunching his scrotum. If he did a thousand rocks back and forth, the image and sheer existence of Gilbert would fade. Finally, he would be alone, just the way he wanted.

What none of his patients, teachers, or acquaintances ever discovered was how unloved he'd felt as a child. His mother never wanted him and his dad ignored him. His mother stuck him in a Vermont boarding school when he was nine. His dad kept Gilbert on a farm he had in Iowa. Twice a year, his mother drove him back and forth to school. She was stoic, and he was happy with that. His whole life he'd been last at everything. They chose him last for every team and sport, excluded from him school cliques because he didn't talk much, and forgot about him because he was barely average at everything he tried.

In community college he was turned down on dates and tuition help, and never asked about his political or religious preferences. In time, he realized that he had no political or religious preferences. His one ability seemed to be in counseling souls more troubled than he was. That's why Vinessa had been eager to have him as a therapist. In retrospect, he now thought she figured he was a DID in the closet. *I'll show her,* he thought.

He spent the next two days on Google Chrome, up on the Surface Web, visible to his ISP, and spreading cookies on websites everywhere. This computer would be left behind in the closet, and would be proof of his good intentions. In truth, he had no good intentions—he had rage. Vinessa's abrupt dismissal brought back painful memories of other attempts at socializing and rebuffs by strong women. He hated that—who in hell do they think they are! He wanted to lash out at the world with the ball peen hammer he'd found in the garage. Instead, he decided to use their own game against them.

He searched the obvious—financial sites, advice columns, investments for the long run, all by investors NOT traders.

The first site he landed on gave good advice for the trail he would be leaving behind. They said, "COVID-19 investing is an effort to conquer uncertainty. It's not just what you feel as an individual either, but also in a collective sense. It's often been said that COVID-19 is both a health crisis and an economic one. That makes it different from any human crisis in the past one hundred years. Against that backdrop, uncertainty is a natural outcome."

Forbes advised, "That's why two personal finance experts just released the new investing episode of our *Friends Talk Money* podcast, Managing Money in a New COVID-19 Economy (available wherever you get podcasts)."

He drove thirty-five miles to Mesa to a used computer store specializing in scrubbed computers for bargain basement prices. Sparki's turned out to be a garage attached to a row house that looked vintage WWII. Sparki herself turned out to be a woman in her fifties, who looked older and smoked constantly. She sold him a well-used Lenovo ThinkPad X270. She said it was worth $200, so he offered her $160 in cash. She said OK, but don't bring it back. "Can I surf on it?" he asked. "Yeah, but it's slow as sand," she said.

He took it back to the Carefree house and spent two hours making it bulletproof. He bought a new VPN on the web with the ThinkPad that he could connect to Central America and "seventy more countries." The VPN sales site guaranteed him allowance to P2P/Torrenting, using 256-bit AES encryption, and best of all, fast and secure access to Vince's VPNs down in the Dark Web. He would get there through his special channel, which would leave no trail for Vince to follow. This is the one he'd boogie with when the time came.

He spent most of that night searching the cloud with his well-used Think Pad, but using the rental house network router. Of course, he reminded himself, there's some risk. To avoid it, he kept his searches general, bouncing around banks and investments in several dozen countries under a safe search string. *The Cook Islands* site jumped out at him.

Picture a paradise where you can be lawsuit-proof. A place to hide your hard-earned assets far from the grasp of former or soon-to-be-former spouses, angry business partners or, if you happen to be a doctor, patients who might sue you. Lawyers drumming up business say they have found just the place: the Cook Islands. And, thanks to a recently released trove of documents, it is clear that hundreds of wealthy people have stashed their money there, including a felon who ran a $7 billion Ponzi scheme and the doctor who lost his license in the Octomom case. These flyspeck islands in the middle of the Pacific would be nothing more than lovely coral atolls, nice for fish and pearls, except for one thing: the Cooks are a global pioneer in offshore asset-protection trusts, with laws devised to protect foreigners' assets from legal claims in their home countries.

He'd need a bank account there, but not yet. After a five-minute search he found the site for the CSB bank. It was in Rarotonga, the main island and provided, through its international license, remotely opened accounts. *No need to go there*, he thought; *good thing—it's a three day trip, by air with no less than three stops.*

While he never wanted to go there, he still needed to be able to travel out of the US without using his American passport. In fact, the more he thought about it, he needed to be someone else. The only real safety he'd have if the world turned on him like Vivian/Vinessa/Vince did was to do what she'd done. He needed to jettison Garrison and become someone else. He needed to be whoever he said he was. That would take a bonafide birth certificate, driver's license, credit cards, Social Security number, and most important a passport with someone else's name and his picture on it.

By dinnertime, he knew he should take no more risks using the rental home's router, even to access his TOR VPNs.

So he drove down the hill from Carefree to a computer café in Tempe called Not Your Big Brother's Gaming Center. The Yelp ad said they gave players of all ages a bang-up gaming experience and environment. They rented their machines by the hour—the chalkboard up front provided machines by names of games and broadband strength—and it varied from four dollars an hour to seven. It was just run down enough to make him think they offered other computer services as well. An orange-haired girl was at the counter, assigning gamers to booths. He waited until no one else was in line.

"Say, I'm looking for a few hours with a machine I can dig down into TOR with. My Mac is on the fritz, ya know. I doan wanna be close to no other dudes and no one peeking over my shoulder either. You got a booth for that?"

She looked at him through watery eyes blackened by a quarter-inch of mascara.

"Yeah, in the back. Ain't a booth, it's like an old-fashioned telephone booth. Heavy machine there, our ISP address and you clear histories, visits, and cookies when you shut down. No cameras in there, know what I'm saying? Twenty bucks for the first hour, fifteen after that. One box of Kleenex in there, use it, right? Garbage sack on the floor."

He gave her a crumpled twenty and looked at his watch.

Once inside the unpainted plywood walls, he could hear sounds from the gaming room behind him. The computer was a desktop under the cardboard table, and the monitor was only 17 inches, not like the big gaming combos out front. But it did the job.

Vince had told him TOR stood for "the onion router." It layered encryption over routing. He said it was like mailing a paper envelope with another envelope inside and so on and on like peeling an onion. "Every onion is an envelope, got it?" he'd asked. Garrison's own research said it was a single entity introduced through relays into the system. They could be both your exit node and your entry point. You had to edit the torrc config file in /Browser/Data/Tor/Torrc. He'd written down the exact path of the config file on the back of a business card from the UPS Store. He also rented a four-inch-square mailbox for $310 per year. Eventually he worked his way down to the files the family had used to create their member's new identity cards, fees, needs, and wants. Oddly, it reminded him of an old-fashioned rolodex.

Once he was that far in, he backed out slowly half way and then wrote new exit nodes into Barbados using this line: RocksListenaddress179 > RocksPort 1212 > ExitNodes {gg}. He was no longer surfing through the open Internet.

What he didn't know yet was that TOR alone would not keep him fully anonymous. Vince had mumbled something about how the effin NSA would someday compromise the TOR network. He was fanatic about using apps that were correctly configured to send Internet traffic through TOR. So Garrison bought the Tor Browser Bundle. It was preconfigured to protect his privacy on the TOR browser itself. TOR encrypted his traffic to and from the TOR network. The final encryption would be done by that last website. That turned out to be the one where he could buy fake passports and every other identity document needed to move in and out of the US to Western Hemisphere countries as and when he needed to. This was his bugout bag.

CHAPTER 15

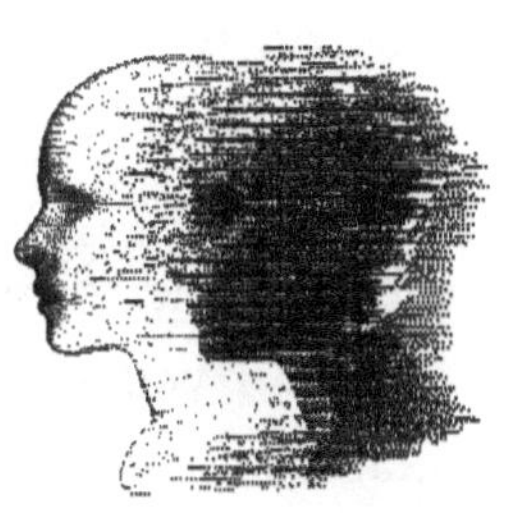

Like any magic trick, fraud depends on making people look at one hand while you use the other against them. Garrison's get-even plan took advantage of one of the oldest financial frauds in the history of financial crime. While still only a draft, he hoped to flesh out the details by reading a book. He went to a half-price bookstore in Scottsdale wearing a large COVID-19 mask, dark sunglasses, and a skullcap over his ears and paid cash for a used copy of *The Wizard of Lies: Bernie Madoff and the Death of Trust*. He'd been in college when the world's largest Ponzi scheme was discovered in New York, and now he hoped to be invisible when his own Ponzi scheme devastated Vinessa and her thirty-six families. He'd bring new meaning to the word "trust" in revocable family "trust." They'd find out trust can disappear just like people can disappear.

Like any financial or mental health problem, he started with a list of first steps. 1. New SSN. 2. New passport—not issued by US—must be English-speaking country. 3. Buy an RV to avoid motels, and restaurants. Use freeways—not back roads—everybody looks at a stranger on a back road. 4. Create new DBA under Emergence Inc. for promotion. 5. Create new LLC in Delaware—use it to create new LLC in Nevada—use the Nevada LLC to open two new bank accounts—one in Cook Islands—one in Jamaica. He estimated one to two weeks to finalize all five steps.

Step 1 was rudimentary. He started by googling fake Social Security cards and found a website that sold blank ones through several form catalogues. If he bought one and put a different name on it, he could be someone else. If it's just your local bank, or Macy's department store, or even a public lending library, he could use it. No one checks. No one can. Well, almost on one. The IRS can check because SSN is used to calculate benefits under the Social Security Act. The feds can because Congress allows them to do that, if authorized by a court order. But there's no photo on SSN cards and no one carries them around anymore. He could just say the number over the phone. He'd soon learn that more often than not, people are just asked for the last four of their social. He'd take care of that.

A fake passport looked impossible until he used his new VPN to create a new TOR channel in the Dark Web. He found several sites selling genuine passports with his own picture on them. It was very expensive, but when the time came he'd have money to burn, he thought. Other sites offered fake international driver's licenses, which he could use alongside his fake passport. That part of identity changing only took money. The more difficult problem was creating a personal history to match the names and the face on his fake identity documents.

To do that, he switched to his Microsoft Edge browser and searched obituary records for white males born on his birthday but who'd died before they turned twenty-one. He had to find legitimate deaths, so he turned to obituaries in newspapers in Cleveland. He found a man born on the same day and year he was. The newspaper pic was close enough and he'd died at nineteen. His name was Lee Stanna Miller. Then, he stole that true-life story, matched it with his own photograph, and manufactured a new identity. He wasn't sure he wanted to be Lee, so he decided he'd be Miller on the road from Arizona to wherever he decided to hide in phase one of his get-outta-Phoenix plan.

The start was getting a shiny new driver's license in a new name in Nevada. That took a two-day trip to Las Vegas. All he did in the MVD office was announce his full name—Lee Stanna Miller. He'd tell them he just moved to Nevada from his home state, Ohio, and had just learned how to drive. He'd smile when they told them this was his first driver's license. He showed them the real birth certificate with Lee Stanna Miller's name on it. He'd conned the hospital into sending him a copy. It wasn't certified, but Las Vegas didn't care. He wore a black suit, a fake black goatee, and horn-rim glasses over the top of his black felt COVID-19 mask.

When he got a quizzical look, he said, "I'm Amish. Our religion objects to modern things like cars and clean shaving."

He passed the driving and written tests and left with a driver's license in a new name but with his picture. Easy.

He could recite his made-up Ohio history by researching the small village where Lee Stanna Miller was born. He would say, if asked, that he went to West Holmes High School just five miles from Millersburg, Ohio, where his extended Amish family lived. He would say he'd gone for one year to University of Akron Wayne College, but didn't like it. Then, he'd worked at Walmart stacking shelves, and then he got a better job with a family that had two taco wagons, but only one son with a driver's license. He really liked that job, he'd say.

Three days before Christmas, his planning was interrupted by *the* phone call. Every year for the last nine years he'd dreaded getting this same infuriating call. *How does the asshole always manage to find my phone number?* He let it ring three times and then clicked ANSWER. He said hello and heard the voice he hated most in the world.

"Garrison, it's Gil."

Gil. Gil the asshole twin brother he wished he didn't have. Gil the twin his double-asshole father liked best. Gil the religious freak who hid his homosexuality under his monastic robe and glowed when parishioners called him Father Gilbert.

"Oh, it's you again," he said, hoping this one would be shorter than last year's call. At least then it only lasted a few minutes because Gil called from his office rather than using his cell phone to make an expensive overseas call.

"How are you, Garrison? I miss you. Did you know it's been seven years since we've even seen one another? I love you, brother, and hope Christ is still in your heart."

"Jesus Christ, Gil, I wish you'd not insult me with religious crap. I'm still the atheist in the family, not that it's much of a family. Heard from dear old Dad this year? He should be getting out on parole sometime, right?"

"Come on, Garrison, let's not talk about him. He's as lost to me as he is to you. And I'm sorry you took my hope as a taunt. I always worry about you. You know that. Is there any chance you could come to New Mexico and see me? I promise not to insult you with religious crap."

"No, Gil, I'm not coming within a thousand miles of Hobbs freakin' New Mexico."

"But Garrison, you're in Phoenix now, aren't you? That's well within a thousand miles and . . ."

"Dammit, Gil, you've been stalking me? Again? How did you know where I was? How do you ever know?"

"I know because God tells me, Gare. Can I call you Gare? Remember when we played hide and seek and we'd switch names? I'd be Gare and you'd be Gil. Remember?"

Against his better judgment, he fell into a conversation with a twin that never liked him.

"That's shit, Gil. We played hide and seek maybe three or four times, and only when Dad came to see Mom and me from Canada. I remember the first time Dad took his belt off. He wacked me because of that stunt you played on him, pretending you were me, and hiding when he came, belt swinging, looking for you. That's what I remember."

"Yes, Garrison. I'm truly sorry for what he did to you and how things turned out. Let's talk about the here and now, though. It's almost Christmas and we had some good Christmases, didn't we? At least a few before Mom died.

Tell me what you're doing now. Still the psychiatrist thing, right?"

"I'm not a psychiatrist; I'm a mental health therapist. You know that. Funny how we both became something we never had as kids—mental health providers. Mom was gone and Dad was nuts. Now you counsel people to let God in their lives. I counsel them to keep God away."

"No, Gare, you don't do that. I hear you're very well liked and you help lots of people."

"What a turd you are, Gil. You don't hear anything about me. We talk once a year and it's always on your dime. Well, that's it. I've got work to do."

"But Gare, you should visit our small monastery here just a few miles from Hobbs. It's a tiny town and has a Catholic middle school. There are three priests here. Two teach in the school, and one says Mass every morning and twice on Sundays. I don't teach or deliver Mass. I just meditate on the Lord's ways and the Devil's intervention. And I write screeds. Some are about you, but most are about me. You are an afterthought. Remember always that I'm the firstborn twin and . . ."

Garrison was impatient to get this over but knew his brother had to show his superiority over all other mortal beings.

"All right, Gil, give it to me again. You call yourself Father Gilbert, but you're not a priest. Explain why you became a monk instead of a priest."

"Priests come from different Catholic religious orders. I was ordained a Franciscan priest but now live a monastic life. Monks live a stark but contemplative life. We don't say mass, hear confessions, or engage parishioners. We engage God. He is our exclusive relationship. We are empowered by the Holy Spirit and spend our days in prayers. We bring to God all those who know not their God, who are lost in self-seeking, who have turned away from truth and love. That's why I call you every year during this holy season and . . ."

Garrison hung up. Not physically, because you can't hang up an iPhone. You just press a little red circle on the screen, and the voice disappears. He wished he could do that to Gilbert—push his little red button.

He waited for the phone to ring again. It always did. He pushed his swivel chair back against the side of the bed and waited. But this year, of all years, Father Gilbert didn't call back. *Good goddamn thing, you asshole priest,* he thought as he wiped the sweat from the back of his neck.

He went back to his yellow pad where he'd doodled in the margins. It was his get-outta-Phoenix list. His doodle was a series of circles interacting with one another like soap bubbles blown through a plastic hoop. He added one more bubble. Find a place to buy Franciscan priest robes, and clerical collars. Get rosary beads and a small beat-up leather bible.

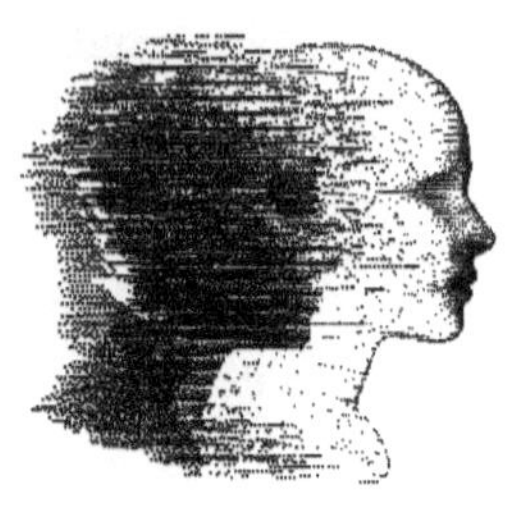

CHAPTER 16

The Bernie Madoff book Garrison bought at half-price was worth about half what he paid for it. It was too complicated. What Bernie had done in New York to his closest friends was slick and worked because his friends trusted him. Just like Vinessa's identity-changing families trusted her. Bernie carried on his fraud for years by making up financial results one year at a time, and convincing friends to give him more and more money to invest. Garrison wanted to set up the fraud, run it for a few months, and then disappear with the money, leaving Vinessa in the dumpster. That simple goal needed a simpler plan than the one Bernie concocted.

All Ponzi schemes have one common essential. They use early investor money to salt more investor money. Bernie used invested money from later investors to fictitiously pay to early investors, who thought they were doing very well.

He paid them above market expectations, and they told their friends. Their friends invested, and he paid them out of fictitious yields on earlier invested money. His Ponzi scheme only worked if enough fresh money came in to pacify earlier investors. Once the inevitable point was reached—not enough new money coming in to fool everybody—the bottom dropped out and Bernie went to jail.

Garrison did not face those problems. He had no intention of constantly looking for new money to pacify investors. His plan was essentially a one-time hit—he'd get as many of the thirty-six families to sign family trust agreements as he, in Vinessa's name, could con. He estimated the front-end take would be about one hundred thousand dollars per family. If that worked, he'd have three and a half million dollars—in Vinessa's name as their trustee. Then since he controlled the bank accounts in her name, he'd drain every nickel. He'd have a chain of offshore banks in place to hop-scotch-wire the money. It would be untraceable, because each name in the chain would be fake. The last one would be his honey bucket. Vinessa would get the angry calls, and he'd watch from an island in the Caribbean, or maybe Polynesia. One and done, as they say in the sports world.

The email on his laptop changed his mood. He went from feeling good to feeling ecstatic. The header said, VALENTINA GUSTAFFSON. The subject line read, GUSTAFFSON FAMILY TRUST. The "to" line had his email address, which all the families thought was hers—Emergence.Inc.trusts@gmail. com. He read it quickly, then again slowly, then a third time with a glass of wine in hand.

Vinessa, this is Valentina. You are good? No COVID? We agree to family trust—you will be our family trustee—that is so? I talk our tax man and he approve. We have real property, but he says we not put that in because of mortgages. We have good cash to run properties. He says not put that in. But he does not know about CDs bonds I have. Remember those? Was your idea. They are in Canadian bank safe deposit box under lock and key. We also have some gold bullion. We can turn both into cash and then wire from our checking account. I think we must turn into cash—$345,000 Canadian. You send us wiring instruction later. First you send family trust agreement for us, Lars too, to sign. We will get 3% return quarterly, yes? CDs pay maybe 1.7%. Gold i don't know. We are ready to sign. Your friend Valentina.

He could hardly believe his eyes—$345,000 Canadian? Holy shit, he thought. That would be about $268,000 US dollars at the current exchange rate of $1.286 inverse. He wrote back,

Thank you Valentina. We are very happy to help you now in this dreadful time of COVID in our country and yours. My assistant, Mr. Garrison Venable, is helping me set up bank accounts and wiring protocols. Please send back the trust agreement he sent to you. Get it signed by a notary first. Wait, I think it's called a Commissioner of Oaths in Canada. Whichever. Send it back. We need it to open an offshore account in your names. Once the account is opened, Mr. Garrison will notify you. The account will pay 3 percent per annum, quarterly, when the bank credits the account. Mr. Garrison will send you either checks or wires for the earnings in the account. I will be the account holder to protect your identity, but the money is yours because the trust is revocable. You know that, right? My Love to your family. Valentina.

This first inkling of success was not just getting the first family to commit to the trust program. It was suggested by how badly he'd may have misjudged the amount of money the Emergence families would be able to raise as they hid from their prior lives. If he got most families to join, and most of them committed what the Gustaffson family just had, his estimates were too low. What if eighty percent committed at the same level? Pursing his lips, he mouthed the words to himself, slowly. Seven . . . million . . . seven hundred seventy-two thousand . . . dollars. Bending toward the monitor, he took his hand off the mouse. Shuddering, he pulled his blue-light computer glasses down and looked over the rims at the typed words. He muttered, "Are you kidding? Impossible!"

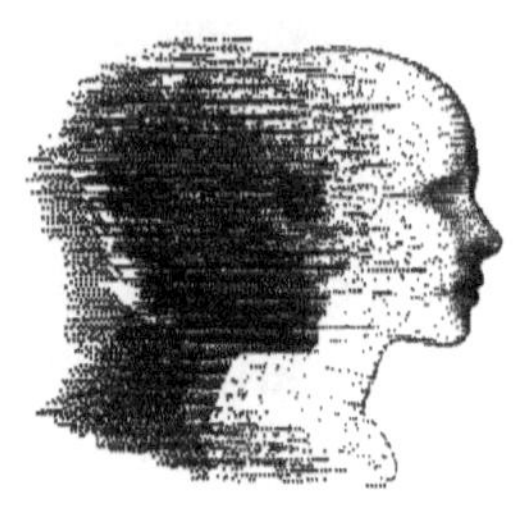

CHAPTER 17

Now that he knew the Gustaffson trust would be funded in just a few weeks, Garrison staged the series of transfers that would make him rich. Like many modern pirates, he investigated the phenom called Bitcoin. For some, Bitcoin was a way to avoid complications with US dollars or German euros. For him, it was purchasing anonymity. The notion came to him as he jotted notes about solutions for the Gustaffson first deposit in some bank somewhere. His yellow pad glowed at him.

How to hide money—buy hosting services anonymously—hide links to real-life banking info—leave no digital track—buy subscription services without revealing personal identity or any data?????

He knew the real answer was to do everything online, which seemed natural given the ongoing COVID-19 surge. No one in their right mind wanted to go into a bank, much less stand in line with strangers whose masks were handkerchiefs. If he did everything online in a corporate name rather than as a person and could find a currency that met his need for absolute secrecy, he could make Gustaffson's money his money.

The first obstacle, he learned, was federal law. The USA Patriot Act forced all financial institutions to obtain, verify, and record information from individuals or companies that opened bank accounts. The weak link in the Patriot Act's chain on American citizens might be Bitcoin. The Internet, or at least the Dark Web, said it was possible to purchase Bitcoins pseudonymously. That word alone, *pseudonymous*, gave him an electric charge as he dug deeper into the Dark Web. He'd used the word in college a few times when writing screeds to newspapers. It was writing under a false or fictitious name. *Sweet Jesus*, he thought, *if I can write secretly, I can invest secretly. Why the hell not?*

Bitcoin is bought and sold out of "wallets." Every Bitcoin has a block chain that records the address of every wallet that has held a specific bitcoin. That made the challenge simple. He had to find a way the wallet could not be connected to him. This is where Vince's advice came in. Dumb shit didn't even know he was helping to set up Vivian for the fall. That was the thing about Vince. He felt he was Vivian and resisted the thought of her aging into Vinessa.

He'd buy Bitcoin only in the Dark Web. The key was to use someone else's laptop. He had that—the $160 well-used

Lenovo ThinkPad he'd bought for cash in Mesa, no questions asked. And he had the NAS alongside it to get to the Dark Web without leaving a trail. He would use someone else's Internet connection, so his ISP didn't show up. And he'd mask it anyhow—that's what Vince told him to do. All he had to do was download http://bitaddress.org.html and he was in, ready to create his anonymous wallet. Once he had a wallet address and a private key, he was in business, but not under his name. It would be a corporate name that was itself a fiction—a legal fiction.

He knew that Vince had originally set up Emergence Incorporated as an LLC in Nevada. They used the name "incorporated" as part of the name even though it never was an incorporated company—it was always a limited liability company. That prompted Garrison to check the public record and find out why so many people were creating LLCs in Nevada rather than the national preference to file in Delaware. The Nevada legislature favored the gaming industry. It fell in line with Las Vegas's marketing slogan. "What Happens in Vegas Stays in Vegas."

People filed there because Nevada had no state income, corporate, or franchise taxes. Garrison didn't care about that—he had no intention of paying taxes anyway. What he liked about the Nevada law was it guaranteed privacy protection for LLCs choosing to be anonymous. He could form it as a single-member LLC without filing operating agreements. Nevada really believed in the corporate veil that protected individuals from liability, and best of all, had no formal information-sharing agreement with the IRS.

So, he created a new LLC in Nevada online under the name *Bladderglaze, LLC*. The genius in it was using Vinessa's name rather than his own as the "incorporating" member. That way, when the chickens came home to roost and someone called the feds, it was Vinessa's name that would show up on a FISA warrant.

Once he had the corporate structure in place, he went online to https://ein-gov-online.com/new/llc, and obtained a tax identification number. The trick there was embedded in the online form. It required him to select a tax classification for the LLC. He chose "individual" so any taxes would be passed through to her. He selected Nevada for the state where the LLC was formed and then put her name on the line for "managing member." And he used her real SSN to complete the form.

The last requirement was to check a box on the bottom of the online form. "By checking this box, I agree to submit the information provided to this website. I agree that I have provided truthful information and that checking this box acts as a signature of my agreement to the terms of use of service. I hereby authorize GovFilings to be my third party designee to submit my completed SS4 form to the IRS, receive my EIN, and to answer questions from the IRS on my behalf."

Then he typed in her name and listed his phone number and his email address. That way, any follow up would come to him, not her. As promised on the government's website, his EIN was delivered to him, although addressed to her by email, "within the hour." Brilliant, he thought. Now he had a tax identification number, which all on and offshore banks required to open new accounts.

The second-to-last piece was to open an account at a legitimate bank under the name *Bladderglaze, LLC*. He'd list Vinessa as the only individual on the account. Any deposits, withdrawals, and online statements would be made by him but identified as coming from her. Even the new tax ID number would be traced back to her, not him. And it would all happen via his email address. He chose the International Bank and Trust in Scottsdale just because of the name on the door. He never saw the door because their website encouraged online account setup. Within the hour of getting the new tax identification number, he had a new cash and checking account at https://fibt.com/.

The irony was delicious, he thought. He was stealing her identity in order to steal money from people she had helped change their own identities. *Sweet*, he mused as he went to the kitchen and uncorked a bottle of Moët & Chandon champagne he'd bought, online, just for this occasion.

CHAPTER 18

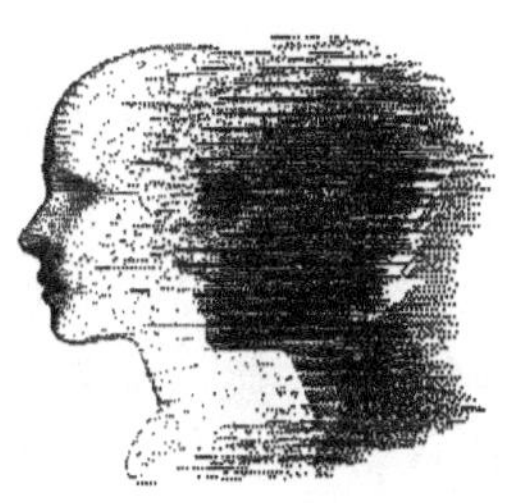

Three weeks later, he got an email from Valentina Gustaffson asking whether he'd received the pdfs of the signed family trust agreements, and whether they could wire the funds to the Emergence Incorporated bank account. He replied that he had the signed agreements and gave them the wiring instructions to transfer the money to the International Bank and Trust account. That afternoon, he checked the online account. The wire transfer had been received but the account noted that funds would not be available for disbursement for three business days. He waited until Friday and checked again. The new account showed a cash balance of $268,000 US dollars. He could hardly believe it. On Monday, he got an email from a bank officer asking whether he needed advice or assistance in investing the cash in either ETFs or mutual funds paying positive dividends and warning him of the inflation that accompanied cash accounts. He didn't answer. He drained the account by buying Bitcoin and moving that wallet to a new one in Panama.

He spent most of every day for the next month creating thirty-three new family trusts from Vinessa's thirty-six Super Zips. Feeling giddy, he sent emails to the remaining non-Super Zip codes, postal codes, and two families living in Hong Kong, who did not have postal codes. Both of the families in Hong Kong opted in and asked for family trust documents. To his utter amazement, eight other families also asked for trust agreements; that gave him forty-one families happily signing trust agreements and then wiring money to what they all thought was Vinessa's bank. He got $48,000 from a family in Nova Scotia. The two Hong Kong families wired $900,000. The total "haul," as he'd started calling it, was $5,207,000.

The results were breathtaking, so much so that Garrison felt the need to create accounts in three other Arizona banks with the word "trust" in the name. Now he had four bank accounts to manage, and in a short time to close. None of the families expected a return until the end of the first quarter following their deposits. In seventy-two hours all of it would be his. Then it would be get-outta-Phoenix time.

He relished the day. With a fresh pot of coffee in the kitchen and his Lenovo Think Pad fired up alongside his Seagate Personal Cloud 2-Bay NAS drive, he dove into the Deep Web to open offshore banks to create hopscotch deposits. Once the 5.2 million dollars was wired out of Arizona banks into the first of the string of offshore accounts, he thought about step two in the game in his head—he called it From Dollars to Bits. He would buy Bitcoins in

London with half the money. That would move two and a half million in Bitcoin into new wallets in Europe and Southeast Asia. He worked feverishly over eleven straight hours, pausing only for bathroom and stretching breaks. He opened accounts at four offshore banks, with the last stop being his already-established personal account in the Cook Islands. He used a London Bitcoin trader, coinbase .com, to shift from US dollars to Bitcoin once the money was out of the Arizona accounts and in the offshore chain of new accounts known only to him. He knew Vinessa would dissolve when she found out, and that Vince would likely soon come out. *Fuck 'em both*, he breathed.

Within hours after getting confirmation from the third bank in the chain, he moved everything to the Cook Islands account. When that famously protective bank answered his email inquiry as to his account status, they wrote back, immediately insisting he "not use email to post inquiry about deposit standing." He was sternly instructed to use his proper logon credentials to review the current holdings. He did that and felt giddy when he saw the balance. The hopscotching around the world had cost him $870 in bank transaction fees, but he was now the sole owner of $5,206,130 in hidden cash and Bitcoin that he'd spend with his new hidden identity, in a foreign country. Screaming at the top of his voice, "Jamaica, here I come!" he got drunk for the first time since college.

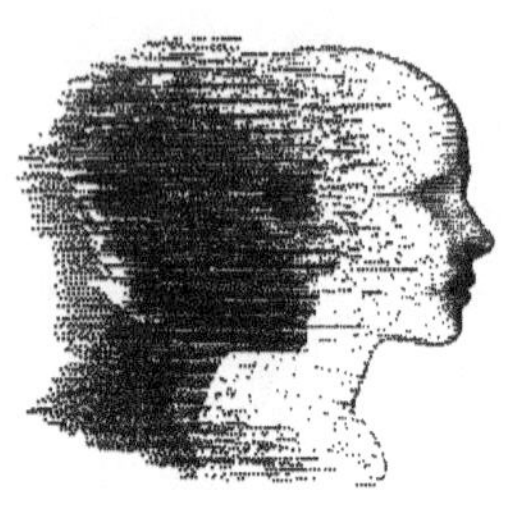

CHAPTER 19

Garrison spent a full day consulting Deep Web sources for ways to disappear. He used the Deep Web rather than the TOR browser to get to the Dark Web. He vaguely remembered Vince's holier-than-thou lecture about the differences among the three levels of the Internet. The Surface Web, dominated by Google, Bing, Mozilla, and other mainstreet browsers indexed all sites and URLs there. The Deep Web was that part of the Internet not indexed or accessed by search engines. It was either password protected or mounted on staging servers. Accessing the Deep Web doesn't require a special browser or unique protocols. Dark Web access came through the encrypted Tor browser. That meant everyone trying to access the Dark Web remains anonymous by default. Ironically, Vince had said it was created by the freakin' US government to hide for military and self-defense purposes. But, he crowed, it's anonymous.

So dudes use it for illegal shit. And that's where Bitcoin was launched.

One Deep Web site said the key to disappearing yourself was to erase all bank accounts, social media contacts, and paper that might suggest his existence. *Check*, he thought. He'd closed his own account at Wells Fargo by withdrawing the $11,200.60 via a certified check payable to himself. Then, four miles away, he cashed that check at a casino on the Salt River Pima reservation for chips. He spent a half hour making stupid bets on a roulette wheel, ending up with $10,875 in chips. He turned those into cash and left wearing the same sunglasses and COVID-19 mask he'd worn at the tables.

For Garrison, the pandemic was a godsend. As he prepared his escape, he wore his mask everywhere and everyone he came close to veered away from him. Police-officer-style sunglasses, hats, and masks allowed him to blend in, with no one being able to describe him as he exited from Phoenix. His baldhead plastic wrapping made his mask and glasses a perfect disguise.

The next piece of advice the disappear site gave was easy. He had a Facebook account that had not been used since he left Australia. Still, he closed it, just in case. Then he dealt with the physical stuff in Vinessa's leased house. He put everything that could identify him into a large plastic garbage bag. His credit cards, Australian driver's license, everything with his name on it went in the bag, including all of his clothes. He kept his Android phone but destroyed the iPhone with the ball peen hammer in the garage. He threw the pieces in the bag.

He didn't bother wiping the house down since his fingerprints were everywhere and he'd never get it perfectly clean. He had two Cricket phones he'd bought with cash while masked and almost indistinguishable from the few people on sidewalks near the store. He bought a half dozen prepaid phone cards at Walmart. One clerk noticed him rubbing his jaw through the mask; it always rubbed him there. He had a ready answer, mumbling and pointing to his jaw—*da da jaw surgy.*

After loading the garbage bag in the trunk, he put his canvas gym bag with his shaving kit, a pint of brandy, and a change of underwear on the passenger seat. He drove nine miles to the closest landfill and threw the bag as far out into the dump pile as he could. Then, never exceeding the speed limit, he drove thirty-five miles south, through Scottsdale on the 101, finally reaching his next planned destination.

He had bought the 2011 Chevy Malibu for $7,200 when he first came to Phoenix. He sold it back to Cactus Jack for $4,100 cash, no questions asked. From there, he used his Cricket phone to call Yellow Cab and told the driver to take him to Apache Junction, almost thirty miles away. The cabbie was sullen but couldn't turn down the fare. He tipped him five bucks when he asked to be dropped off at the Ace Hardware store on West Apache Trial.

Once the cab was out of sight, he walked south ten blocks and reached the Rock Sunshine Travel and RV Center, where he'd rented a cheap space at a monthly rate of $140. Two weeks earlier he'd bought a 1994 Monaco Safari Trek RV for $13,000 cash in Mesa, without showing his driver's license. The salesman asked for his license and said they could not sell a car without confirming that the buyer was licensed. Garrison offered him $500 more than the price pasted to the window screen, $12,500 and paid in cash. He could almost see the salesman pocketing the extra $500 before taking him inside to the finance guy, who documented the sale.

He knew he had to have insurance that would be good in every state. That turned out to be easy. He logged on to AA Insurance, asked for a basic auto quote good everywhere, and filled in all the blanks on the page. He used his new Nevada driver's license number, the Arizona plates on the Monaco Trek, and the address of a Starbucks he saw in Tempe. They emailed him a pdf with his good-to-go insurance card. He stuck it in the glove compartment with his flashlight and a box of Tums.

The Trek looked well used, had a few dents, and scaling paint on the front end. He hoped that made it look not worth stealing or breaking into. It had a Triton V-10 Gas Motor, two twin beds, a working fridge, propane stove, and a rear bathroom. He canceled his rental space, drove the faded yellow RV through the front gates, and turned east onto US 60 toward the Atlantic Ocean. *Perfect*, he thought, *hope it gets me to Key West*.

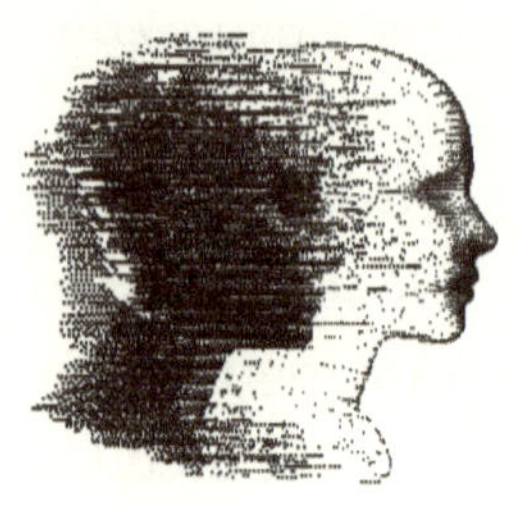

CHAPTER 20

Two weeks later on a Monday morning, Vinessa got a phone call from the leasing agent in Carefree. She didn't recognize the number and there was no caller ID, but the area code, 480, was assigned to Carefree, Arizona. She had not tried to reach Garrison by phone since their last call almost five weeks ago. She assumed it was him.

"Hello," she said softly.

"Hello," the caller said. "Vinessa, is this you?"

"Who is this?" she said cautiously because the voice was female.

"Vinessa, this is Ida. I'm the real estate agent on the lease property you have in Desert Mountain."

"Oh, yes, Ida. We never met, and I'm sorry I forgot your name. Is something wrong?"

"I don't know," Ida said. "Apparently you're not at the house, right?"

"No, not at the moment. I'm on a trip out of state," Vinessa said, wondering if there was any way this woman could know she was in Victoria, Canada.

"Oh, that explains it. I just got off the phone with a deputy sheriff over in Cave Creek. I guess a neighbor called in for a well-person check at the rental property. He said the yard lights were on in middle of the day, and one of the bubblers in a plant had burst and was leaking water out onto the street."

"Oh, my goodness. I have been away and my assistant is in the house. Is he OK?"

Ida took a moment before answering in a cautious tone.

"Well, I just don't know. The officer said he looked in the windows; you know there are a lot of windows. He saw weeds and debris blown up onto the front steps. No one seemed to be inside. He told me the pool in the back looked green, like the chlorine balance was way off. Have you talked to your assistant recently?"

"No, I haven't. Actually, I've been getting some treatments and so he didn't want to bother me," she said, lying.

"Should I call the officer back and meet him at the house? Maybe your assistant is sick, or worse. You know. COVID-19? I can do that if you like."

"No, that won't be necessary. I'll take of it. Someone will go to the house tomorrow and check things. Thank you ever so much for calling."

She clicked the red circle with the little white old-fashioned telephone in it but nothing happened. Her fingers tingled and she had trouble swallowing. A half-empty bottle of water was on the counter, so she drank part of it and part dribbled down over her blouse. Trying to focus seemed impossible, but she managed to go back to her iPhone and search her contacts list. She had only the one mobile number for Garrison. She dialed and heard the ominous response. "This number is no longer in service." She called 411 and they said they had no number for a Garrison Venable.

Feeling anxious, but not really worried, she called her bank contact at Wells Fargo in Seattle and asked if there had been any activity in her personal checking account. They said there had been only two transactions in the last two weeks. Both were checks she wrote. She knew Garrison had given her a form to sign that would open a new Phoenix checking account with Chase Bank under the corporate name *Emergence Inc.* He'd said they would need a small account for basic costs "attendant" to the new family trust arrangements.

It was online, and she'd given him a check for $100 to open the account. She called their number, identified herself, and asked if there had been any transactions recently. They asked for the PIN number. She didn't have it. She asked for a manager. Someone named Charles something came on the line five minutes later. He was sorry, but without the PIN number he could not verify transactions. She asked him whether she was the only person authorized to make changes. He told her to hold the line. A few minutes later he said she was the only authorized signer on the account. Relenting on the PIN issue, he said the only activity had been a PIN ATM withdrawal for $99 dollars. Then he lectured her about fees because the one dollar left in the account was well below their minimum and . . . she rang off on the red button.

Two hours later, after a glass of wine and some saltine crackers, she got up the nerve to call Valentina Gustaffson at her home in Alberta.

"Hello," a woman with a heavy accent said. " Vinessa, is this you? How wonderful of you to call."

"I am sorry to bother you, my friend," she answered, hoping her voice didn't give away her anxiety.

"I'm in The Empress on Victoria Island and just thought I'd call since we're both in Canada. I don't think we've ever been in the same country at the same time in all the years we've known one another. How is Lars, and how are you?"

"We're fine my dear. The COVID has not visited us. Of course Lars is pacing around waiting for your wonderful Garrison to call us back. We wired him our money for the family trust account there in Arizona. He said it would take a week or two to get everything set up. That was three—no, it is almost four weeks now. He is so excited to get 3 percent on our money. You might remember how stingy he is with money. Is there anything wrong?"

"No, I'm only calling because we are both in the same country for once. It was just a whim. I'm sure you'll hear from Garrison soon."

They made small talk for a few minutes. Vinessa said someone was knocking on the door and it was probably room service. She mouthed a hurried *addio* and hung up. She called the house number for the rental in Arizona and got another out-of-service message there. Stumbling, she nearly fell, tripping over the rug on the floor between the sitting room and the bedroom. She'd been in a suite at the Empress Hotel in Victoria for a month now. She made it into the bedroom and fell face down on the bed with her hands plastered on both sides of her head. She wailed until she blacked out.

When the housemaid used her key to come into the suite the next morning, she'd be surprised to find Vinessa gone but most of her clothes still on the rod in the closet. A day later when the room was empty for two days, the front desk manager had her credit card on file, so he debited her bill and checked her out. They put her belongings in guest storage.

Nine hours after Vinessa's call to Valentina, Vince landed at Sky Harbor Airport in Phoenix and rented a car for the drive up to Desert Mountain to confront Garrison. He found the same weeds and dirt blown up on the front steps, the green swimming pool, and no sign of Garrison.

"You shitty bastard—*bastard*!" he screamed, once he used Vinessa's key to get in and learn Garrison was gone.

He took his time searching the main house, the casita in back, and found absolutely nothing that suggested Garrison had ever been there. The bed sheets in the casita were perfect, but those in the guest room in the main house were untucked, and the pillows were on the floor. Every wastebasket was clean, and nothing was in the garbage cans inside the front fence. The refrigerator was empty, except for a quart bottle of still water in one door pocket. There was dust, but the windows were all closed. The AC was on low. No lights were on inside. The telephone worked. Vince checked the router and network adapter. They both were on, and no devices were plugged in. The TV signal was intact, as was the Cox home telephone system. The house alarm system was turned off. The dishwasher was empty as was the washing machine in the mudroom between the garage and the hallway.

He called Ida's number and told her he was Vinessa's brother and he'd be staying in the house for a week or two. He asked her to call the front gate and make sure they'd let him in and out. They'd let him in because he insisted he was the homeowner's brother and showed them the key to the front door, which he'd found in Vinessa's purse at the Empress. A uniformed security guard followed him to the house. He went back outside and got his backpack from the passenger seat of the rental. It was the only expensive thing he owned—it had a solar pack, multiple slots for laptops and peripherals, USB and HDMI cords, and an external hard drive, which doubled as his NAS device. The extra pair of jeans, two long-sleeved hoodies, three pairs of socks, and two pairs of underwear were stuffed in the bottom of the pack. Everything he needed to find the bastard-*bastard*, he thought.

First thing, he powered up his computer, plugged in the NAS with an Ethernet cable, connected the external hard drive through a USB port, and used his four-letter PIN to get past the Mohave desert scene he used as background. The desert always comforted him—it was arid, lonely, and desolate. *Just like me*, he mumbled. Largely unaware of other people, Vince had always talked to himself. *Who else would listen?* he asked himself.

Using the protocols and pathways he'd memorized years ago, he navigated his way down the TOR browser to his many private VPNs and data collection sites. For him, the Dark Web was not an illicit or dangerous place. He loved it because nothing there was indexed. That protected him and his data from open Internet search engines like Google. He had locked down all Emergence Incorporated files four years ago. But he had given Garrison navigation access and limited logon access. His first job now was to cancel out that bastard-*bastard*. Fortunately, he'd built in special blocks to prevent web crawlers from phishing their way in.

He hoped he could track whatever mischief Garrison had done to Emergence Incorporated files and was stunned to find that nothing looked amiss. He checked all his original data files for changes using the history tab in settings. It would easily define subtle changes. The financial data was the same as it was before he'd given Garrison access. So once he blocked Vince out, the data was safe, again, and unchanged. The nearly $800,000 in the brokerage account was intact. There had been no withdrawals, but there had been a dozen dividend payments on equities and the NAV on the mutual funds looked steady.

WTF is this guy doing? he thought. Then, like the moon coming up out of a black eastern sky, it hit him. *Garrison didn't take or build anything from my data in my VPN channel. He used my path to dig down. Then the fucker musta built a new substructure of own, one I can't see. It's got to be for those freakin' family trusts. And they're not indexed either. Amazing,* he thought. *A dork therapist is using the Dark Web to hide shit from us! I'm gonna red duct-tape his ass to an acid vat.*

The age-old psychiatric question in dissociative identity disorders was whether an alter could be aware of therapeutic efforts with the dominant personality state. Vinessa had been in therapy for at least two years, first with Dr. Estancia in Houston and later with Garrison in Sydney. If some level of communication or memory existed between Vinessa and Vince, it might affect Vince's violent thoughts about Garrison. He would have sensed that violence, even at the nascent stage, would influence Vinessa's own reactions toward Garrison. One thing would have been clear to any therapist treating Vince—he had at the very least an antisocial personality disorder. Was he also homicidal? Psychopathic?

Vince's discovery of Garrison's meddling in the Dark Web made him tense, sweaty, and think about pain. The tendons on his neck stood out as rage set in. He spent the next five minutes surfing the Open Net for the most vicious acid in the world. He found an article on the dangers of using fluoroantimonic acid. It said, "If a worker in the plant were to accidently drop a small quantity of fluoroantimonic acid on his or her hand, it would in seconds eat through the skin, tendons, and ligaments to the bony structure, which it would devour within thirty minutes."

"Okay," he muttered, "you shithead, I'm gonna get my red duct tape, a fifty-five gallon barrel half-full of fluoroantimonic acid, and stuff you in it. I'll hear you scream and laugh my head off as the acid eats you from the inside out."

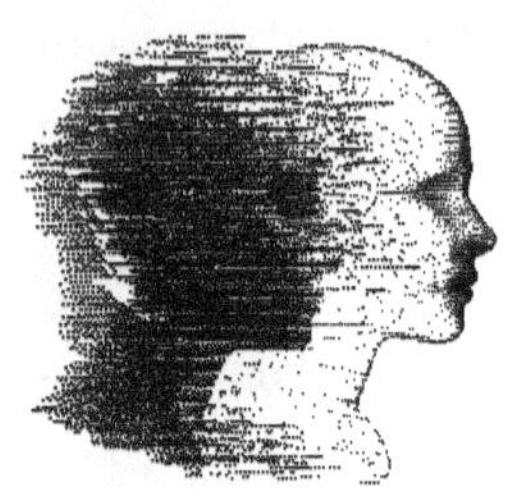

CHAPTER 21

Garrison heard a faint clicktey-click from the engine well as he pulled out of the RV park and headed toward US 60 just a few blocks away. He worried because he knew nothing about how an engine should sound. He'd never owned a new car, but this twenty-six-year-old engine sounded like it might be coming apart. He turned off US 60 onto AZ 79 to get to Tucson. On the way down he passed the Arizona State Penitentiary at Florence. He tried not to look at it as he drove by, five miles under the speed limit.

An hour and twenty minutes later he found a Costco in Tucson, just two miles from the on-ramp onto Interstate 10, the freeway he'd be on for the next week or two. Inside Costco he discovered they wouldn't let him buy anything because he wasn't a "member." He paid cash for the $60 dollar annual membership and said his name was Jay Doe. He gave them a phony address he made up on the spot. They didn't ask for an ID card but they had one for him. It was a thin business card with the name J. Doe on it. *Dumb shits*, he thought. *They can't even spell a fake name right.*

Once inside the giant two-story building, he stopped at the men's room and then selected a large four-by-four flatbed metal cart. Most of the customers were wearing masks except for the men wearing MAGA Hats. He avoided both, and also avoided the aisles where MAGA guys piled up their carts. He filled his cart with two cases of bottled water, a case of Coors Lite, sixty cans of various meats, soup, dried fruits, sardines, tuna, chub mackerel, Hunt's tomato sauce, corn, pitted olives, a dozen bags of dehydrated foods, trail mix, beef jerky, sugar, coffee, dried beans, corn chips, six packs of soft drinks, extra-large bags of candy, two loaves of bread, condiments, four quarts of motor oil, two gallons of anti-freeze, a new electric coffee pot, a frying pan, a two-quart aluminum cooking pot, four boxes of double-A batteries, two flashlights, two new pillows, a set of sheets, a heavy wool blanket, two pair of Levis, a Levi jacket, two baseball hats, four T-shirts, two sweat-style hoodies, a set of plastic dishes, a box of plastic knives, forks, and spoons, six rolls of toilet paper, and a large pack of paper towels. As a last minute pick, he grabbed a large watermelon off a stand at the start of the long line of shoppers waiting for a checkout slot to open. He paid cash.

On his way out, a bored employee checked the bags, boxes, and bottles on the cart against his check out slip, marked it with a yellow sharpie, and waved him to the exit door. He stopped at the trashcan just outside the door and dropped his new member card and the paid cashier's slip into it. It took fifteen minutes to offload everything into drawers and cabinets inside the RV. He gassed up at a Chevron next to the freeway, paid cash, and eased the wobbly RV onto the freeway. He had almost gotten used to the side-to-side wobble of the giant box on wheels he was now driving.

Next stop, he thought, looking at the map on his Android phone: Lordsburg, New Mexico. When he got there, he gassed up and decided to cut the watermelon. But all he had was a plastic eating knife.

He'd buy a real knife when he crossed the New Mexico border into El Paso, Texas.

CHAPTER 22

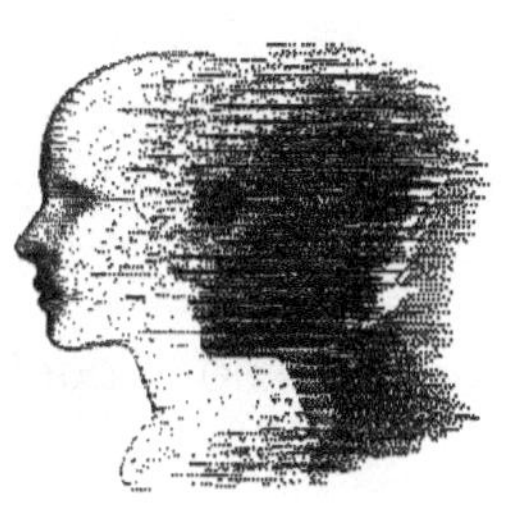

As Vince smoldered in the casita now vacated by Garrison, his mind wandered between finding Garrison and killing him. He was good with technology but actually finding someone was not his strength. Maybe there *was* an answer on the Open Net. His search for skip tracers found people who tracked down deadbeats and alimony slackers. He expanded the search to private investigators. The first half-dozen were an easy delete. When Mozilla found sherlock_sleuths.com, he smiled for the first time in hours. The "About Us" tab sounded perfect.

When you need to find a person for legal or personal reasons, hire us. We have a 100% guarantee. We are not cheap. But if we take your case and fail to find whoever you're looking for, we refund your retainer 100%. We can find anyone, anywhere, because we search millions of records, use both human and artificial intelligence, and have been in business for twenty years. Our clients are hundreds of satisfied public and private persons, corporations, government agencies, universities, and healthcare systems. Everything is confidential, encrypted, and double-checked by onsite private investigators in every state and several foreign countries. When you want the best, contact us online through our website. We do not take phone calls or personal visits. Everything we do for you is done online on the Open Net, or if you prefer on other less visible VPNs and encrypted channels via by closed net pathways.

"Holy shit!" Vince shouted when he found them on the Open Net. He logged off, then back on, and accessed the Dark Web via his VPN.

Once on the Sherlock Sleuths site, he clicked on the chat tag and spent five minutes chatting with a computer's AI interface.

He chatted what he wanted: "A first-rate investigator to find a person for a corporate fraud in the six-figure range."

The return chat line read, "We would be honored to help you find a person."

He typed, "Yes I need you to find a person. How does this work?"

"We find persons based on your particular needs and timing."

"Look, I get AI. But I want to talk to a human on the telephone."

"Call 855-617-5050. A registered private investigator will answer your call. Select option 6 and hit #."

Vince pulled his Android from his back pocket, thumbed in the number, got what looked like a digital switchboard, selected the option, and waited. In seconds a deep male voice said, "Good evening, sir or madam. How may Sherlock Sleuths assist you?"

"Yo," Vince said, "you guys are on it. Jeeze Louise, this was fast service."

"I have your iPhone number on my screen. My name is Clayton Unswor, call me Clatch, everyone here does. To whom am I speaking?"

Vince spent the next fifteen minutes with Clatch. Throughout the call, he kept popping Reese's Thins in his mouth and sucking on his sixteen-ounce Kill Cliff Ignite energy drink. The whole time he was thinking, *These guys are grade triple-X; they'll find the bastard-bastard for us.*

Clatch helped him open an online account. Vince gave Clatch a short version of who Garrison Venable was and why he was looking for him. He explained Garrison's employment by his sister at Emergence Incorporated. Clatch asked for specifics on Garrison's embezzlement of maybe a half a mill—his sneaking away from Phoenix, Arizona, maybe as long ago as ten days—and Garrison's background in finance and mental therapy.

Clatch asked if Vince had a photo. He said no.

Clatch said, "Is this your man?" as an image appeared on Vince's monitor.

"Holy shit, you guys are freakin' amazing. That's him! That's Garrison Venable."

"Yeah," Clatch said, "I just made an ID file on him. Born in Rochester, New York. Catholic, straight, education at SUNY Albany, then online masters in counseling—not impressive source—living in Australia. Therapist—decent clinic—gets $28 Australian per hour—limited benefits. Does all that match up with your guy?"

"He was in Australia. He was my sister's therapist. But in Phoenix, he worked for us—that is, Emergence Inc.—as a comptroller for the last few months. We think he bugged out while the boss of the company was on a business trip away from Phoenix."

"What's the boss's name and what is your role in the company?"

He gave Clatch a partially accurate name for the boss. "Let's call her Vinessa Doe. My name is Vince Doe. I'm her brother and the CTO at Emergence Incorporated."

Clatch laughed, "Got it, man. We're good with alias names. But we need good ole American money as a retainer. And before we get to details, have you called the police, or the FBI? You said your man scooted with maybe a half a mill, right?"

"So, Clatch, here's the thing. We do not want the police or the feds in on this. We are a very private company, and we have people who would go bananas if this becomes public. This is embezzlement, but the source of the money is . . . well, how do I put it? We have members, and their money is private. They are private. So, we need to catch Garrison ourselves. No police. Especially no FBI. OK?"

"Sure, we'll find your man. When we do, we'll tag him with a photo/video set-up, and baby sit him until you catch up. Then, you either call the cops or do with him as you want. We don't arrest or prosecute. We just find people."

"Good to know," Vince said. "Now about the amount this bastard made off with—thing is, we don't really know right now. My guess is a half a mill, but finding out exactly how much is something I'm working on. We need to get on his ass yesterday. Your site says we get a 100-percent guarantee you find our man, or we get our retainer back. How much you calling for as a retainer?"

"Standard is twenty-five thousand now, as retainer money. Plus out-of-pocket expenses added in later for warrants, photography, small bribes to low lifes, snitches, and nosy neighbors. And bullets if we have to shoot your man."

"Shit, man, the twenty five cay is a done deal, but bribes and bullets? You kidding me?"

"Just kidding on the bullets. We find 'em. We don't kill 'em. We are serious on the money and the bribes. A case like this one—with at least five hundred cay in your man's pocket might make him hard to track. We'll get him, no doubt about that. Our PIs are all registered gun owners, with lots of range time, and they conceal-carry full-time. Your account is now open. Wire the retainer with the instructions on your screen in the pdf that's on its way to you. I'll give you an email update every twenty-four hours. This guy's got no police record, no known experience in criminal activity, no addictions, and lots of dough to buy hideouts. But he's pure amateur. Your company must have really pissed him off, but we'll get him. I'd say two days out. OK, you down on all this?"

"I'm down on it, Mr. Clatch; the money will be in your account in an hour. I got to clear this with the boss."

"It's Clatch, not Mr. Clatch. Don't call me Mister. You trying to ruin my reputation in the trade? I'll be back at you tomorrow night about this time."

Vince wired the money a few minutes later. As he leaned back away from the monitor, he still had Garrison's picture up on the screen. He never looked at the asshole while he was teaching him about the Dark Web. Now he took a long look. The picture was like an annual headshot in a manila-colored frame with little squiggly marks on all four sides. He had a long face; kids probably called him horse face. He was porcelain white with pussy lips and big eyes. Probably wore glasses but took them off for the picture, Vince thought. He looked like a choirboy, well-scrubbed, the kind that girls took one look at and thought he was a gay caballero. The pic was black and white, but Vince remembered his hair was reddish-brown and close-thatched. His eyes were black on the monitor but he vaguely remembered his pupils were small, not big like boxers' or wrestlers'. The pic was stern, not a hint of a smile. Vince couldn't remember him ever smiling, but something in his memory fought that thought. *Shit*, he thought, *Vinessa must have liked him. She paid him well, and offered him a big god-dammed salary for the stupid family trust thing. No matter*, he thought as he logged off for the night. *We're coming to get you, shithead. Me and the man called Clatch.*

CHAPTER 23

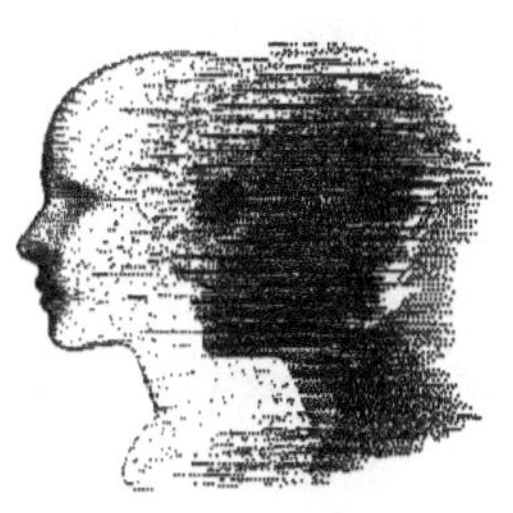

Garrison felt odd to be in El Paso, partly because it was all new to him and partly because his twin brother Gilbert was only a couple hundred miles north, in Hobbs, New Mexico. He'd only talked to him once, on the phone, in the last year. He couldn't remember exactly how long it'd been since he'd seen him, but it'd been a while. What were the odds, he wondered as he pulled of I-10 and into the city center, that he'd run into Father Gilbert. *Freakin Priest!* Just for the pleasure of it, he imagined showing up at Father Gilbert's monastery near Hobbs and surprising him. Would he look older since his entire existence consisted of following his vows of chastity, poverty, and piety? He knew his twin didn't mingle with others, didn't teach, deliver mass, or otherwise interact with humanity. The freakin priest had once described the monastery as four adobe huts, a barn, two mules, a chicken coop, and a church. He said one adobe hut was his and that's all God wanted him to have.

Pulling into a Love's truck stop, he waited in line for an easy bay to navigate a gas pump. With his engine running, but in park, he clicked his phone and checked the COVID-19 status. El Paso had 86,792 positive COVID-19 cases and 1,010 deaths since March 2020. He could see most people there were wearing masks, but not all. It was Texas, after all. He gassed up, washed the windshield, and used the men's. He bought two doughnuts and a large black coffee and asked the bony attendant where the closest sporting goods store was, you know, one that sells hunting stuff.

"Well, there's a one on the east side of town. It's called *Shoot 'Em*, or something like that," the man said in a hoarse voice through his loose fitting mask. "I ain't never been there. If you're looking for a cheap gun, talk to Shorty next door in the tire shop. He's got one he tried to sell me last week. I already got two, what would I need with another one?"

Garrison had checked on Texas gun laws. They didn't require permits, background checks, or a license of any kind. You just had to be over eighteen to buy a long gun and over twenty-one to buy a handgun. He pulled out of the pump line and wobbled the RV next door to a Discount Tire shop. He went into the working part of the store where two cars were up on hydraulic lifts.

"I'm looking for Shorty," he said to the man with the dirtiest hands he'd ever seen. Without looking at him, the man shouted, "Shorty! Pilgrim here looking for you."

Shorty turned out to be well over six feet tall, brown as a walnut tree, and wearing heavy gloves but no mask. As he walked from the back of the shop, he took his work gloves off and pushed up a denim mask over his nose.

"I'm Shorty, whadda ya'll need?"

"I'm Miller," Garrison said, liking the sound of his driver's license name as he readjusted his own mask. "The cashier at Love's said you had a gun you were looking to sell, cheap. Is that right?"

"Hell yeah, Miller. See, times are hard around here. We hear Discount Tire will go out of business. Due to COVID, they say. People are staying home, so who needs new tires? Anyways, I'm letting go of some of my collection. You a hunter or just looking for protection from the drug cartels across the Rio Grande?"

Garrison thought a moment before answering. He had been thinking about a pistol because he'd be parking in open spaces sometimes and in KOA Campgrounds when he could find one. On the spot, he picked a gun he'd seen on a Turner Classic Movie starring Clint Eastwood—a .44 magnum.

"Ah," he paused. "Maybe a .44 magnum. I never had a gun, but I'm starting a long trip through Texas by myself and will be camping out quite a bit. My dad used to have a gun, but he took it with him when he ran off with a floozie; that's what my mom said. They got divorced, and Mom got me."

"Yeah, man that's the shits. I don't have a .44 but I got a stubby .357. Know what that is?"

"No."

"Mine is a Taurus .357 magnum revolver. They call 'em stubby because the barrel is only two inches long. Funny looking, but a damn serious piece of work. It's got a leather poly grip with an oxide finish. Holds five rounds. Weighs about twenty ounces. You can shoot it single or double action. Know what that means?"

"No, I've never fired a gun," Garrison said as he adjusted his mask to keep his words from flowing up into his nose. "Shorty, I gotta tell you the truth here. I know shit about guns. I just think it might be a good idea around a campground. They say you never know. Any way I could try it out before buying? I don't want lessons or anything; it's just that I'm careful, ya know?"

"Hey man, I get that. Shooting a gun the first time is a hoot, but it scares the crap out of some people. My stubby is a little gun, but at .357 it's got a boom that'll wake the whole block up. See, I bought it for a girlfriend who worked a bar and closed up every night. She wanted it to get her from the front door to the parking lot. But she didn't work out and I'm stuck with the gun. I can't show it to my friends."

"Why not? Is there something wrong with it?"

"Hell no. It's just a little bitty thing, and my compadres would make jokes about little bitty things."

"How much would you charge me?"

"Tell you the truth, I paid $329.99 for it and only fired it one time at the gun range. They smirked at it there too. I'll let you have it for three hundred cash."

"I can do that," Garrison said.

"All right. There's a gun range on San Antonio Ave about four miles from here. What's say we meet up there after I get off? I'll bring the gun, show you how to load it, clean it, aim it, and be careful with it. You can fire it and then buy your own ammo at the store. I only have the four shells in it now."

"Four? I though you said it holds five?"

"Yeah, but if you carry it loaded, don't keep a slug under the firing pin. That's what the double action is for. I'll explain it at the range."

"All right, Shorty, you got a deal. I'll bring the cash. What's the street address so I can google it? I'll meet you there. What time did you say?"

Shorty gave him the time and address for the Shoot 'Em Up range and gun store. Garrison showed up on time. Turns out, Shorty liked to talk and he was a damn good shot. They spent a half hour at the range, and Garrison left with gun oil on his hands and feeling like a gangster. The muscular woman with the buzz-cut hair behind the counter told him he ought to buy "home defense shells" for a little girl's gun like that Taurus.

"I assume you're giving the gun to your girlie. She'll be best served with the Remington HTP .357 Magnum 110 Grain SJHP. Shoots a 110-grain bullet at a muzzle velocity of 1295 fps. It has excellent high terminal performance, ensuring maximum effectiveness with proper shot place-ment. Like between your legs if you can't keep your pants zipped when she's not around."

Garrison left El Paso at eight o'clock that night and drove 120 miles to Van Horn, Texas. It was almost midnight when he got there. The Love's truck stop was open, so he pulled in and found a wide space in the back, intending to gas up in the morning. He stumbled over boxes, fell into bed with his clothes on, and slept until the sun was in full bloom through the back window. He got up and went into the three-by-four-foot bathroom. He was taking a leak when someone banged on the passenger door.

"Hey, inside there. You can't just park here. Didn't you see the sign—No Overnight Parking? You ain't out of here in ten minutes and I'm calling the cops."

He zipped up, washed his hands, brushed his teeth, and drove out of the rear parking lot to the gas pumps out front. After filling up the twenty-four gallon tank, he went inside to buy some ice and was surprised to find an I-Hop-Express inside. He felt grungy and hungry so he found a seat, unmasked himself, and ordered the All-American Breakfast—eggs like you like 'em—home fries or grits—choice of meats—coffee and juice—$8.95. A half hour later, he went to the counter to pay his bill and asked the slightly chubby Mexican woman behind the cash register if there was a KOA nearby.

"Don't know about KOA, but if you'll turn around you can see the Mountain View Park, just the other side of the freeway. They have a small swimming pool, a fake putting green, and many open spaces with water, electricity, and a Wi-Fi hook-up that reaches most of the lots."

"Do they take overnighters?" he asked.

"Well, they used to have a one-week minimum, but the COVID has dumped on everything normal in Texas. Carmelita is the manager. Expect she'd take anybody in these days. I live there. It's all clean except the pool."

He drove across the freeway over-ramp and pulled in. Carmelita was a black woman about sixty with a relaxed smile and droopy eyes. She asked how long he might be staying. He told her two nights and gave her sixty dollars.

He picked a lot in the last row. There were no other trailers back there and the view of the Texas panhandle was good. The Wi-Fi was even better.

He parked like he knew what he was doing. Then he figured out how to plug the electric in, attach the water line, and log into the Mountain View network. Once he found the MVs internet access app, he dropped down into the Dark Web and checked his accounts, alerts, and history. All looked like it was supposed to look. He logged off, shut down, and waited thirty seconds. Then he logged back on, accessed Mozilla's browser on the Surface Web, and spent the rest of the day watching CNN and local news from San Antonio.

He'd booked two days because he needed to reorganize the inside of his sixteen year-old Safari Trek. His Costco boxes were stacked up in the kitchen area on the floor and in the bedroom on the opposite side. He'd mastered the sway and roll of the boxy RV, but this was the first time he'd taken a look at his traveling hide-away. He was surprised to find his Safari Trek had its own Wikipedia page.

The Safari Trek was a line of motorhomes built by the Safari Motorcoach Corporation (SMC) based out of Harrisburg, Oregon. The Trek line was developed in the late 1980s. The early pre-Monaco Treks now hold a venerated status among Safari RV enthusiasts—"Trekkies." This is in part due to the Trek's patented "Electro-Majic Bed," which provided for spacious floor plans. There was as well an exceptionally high build quality that used

a riveted aluminum outer skin in lieu of the more
popular tin or fiberglass, real hardwood cabinetry,
and a small-bus-like design that made the Trek
easy to drive and maneuver.

Whadda ya know about that? he thought. No wonder
Carmelita welcomed him. He was a *Trekkie* now. In short
order, he realized why they'd been so popular two decades
ago. There were small closets, drawers, and cubbyholes
everywhere inside. Outside, below the carriage, there were
four large storage bins, a closed rack for the propane tank,
and one for the generator. He was surprised to find lawn
furniture, jacks, toolboxes, spare batteries, shovels, tow-
ropes, chains, and two long rubber hoses. In one large box
he found old kitchen utensils, including a cutting board
and a twelve-inch carving knife. *Now, I can eat the damn
watermelon,* he thought. There were two brooms, some oil
rags, and a large bottle of Windex, all of it stored below the
floorboards. The generator looked fairly new, well maybe
not new, but it was not the original. There was even a spare
propane tank, securely locked in a metal box, that was just
the right size, with pads on the side.

It took two hours to organize everything and get it all
tied down. By five o'clock he was finished. Everything was
freshly Windexed, and he was ready to cook his first meal.
He almost always cooked for himself and had the basics
down pat. He fried the Spam, heated up canned spinach,
and sliced and fried the potatoes, with the skins on. He
drank two cans of Coors Lite, with Saltine crackers, and
sliced the watermelon for dessert.

Then before his stomach growled, he settled in to watch the *Rachel Maddow Show*. She was bright and cheery when she talked about Trump's latest outburst, morose when she reported on the New York COVID numbers, and consistently repetitive about both issues. After forty minutes of the fifty-minute program, he hit exit and found a movie on his Netflix app. He liked action movies where thousands of bullets whizzed by, the good guys won, and the bad guys died. *Serves 'em right,* he thought.

He pulled out of Van Horn the next morning, waving bye to Carmelita as he went through the gate. She shaded her eyes and squinted at him. He had his mask on. So far, no one, except the cashier at Loves, had seen him in his three-day drive without his mask, sunglasses, and a hat. He changed hats at every stop. Next stop, Houston. Google said it was 626 miles east on I-10. He would have to find another KOA park. He'd promised himself he'd never drive one mile over the speed limit or do anything to draw attention to himself. *Goddamn,* he thought, *COVID is good for something—masks—social distancing—keeping to yourself.* He remembered that site he'd found about disappearing. Always use cash—don't talk to anyone—keep disguised—don't stay long in any one place—stay on the move until you get to a safe place. That, he thought, would take another week, and then a short boat trip from Key West to Jamaica.

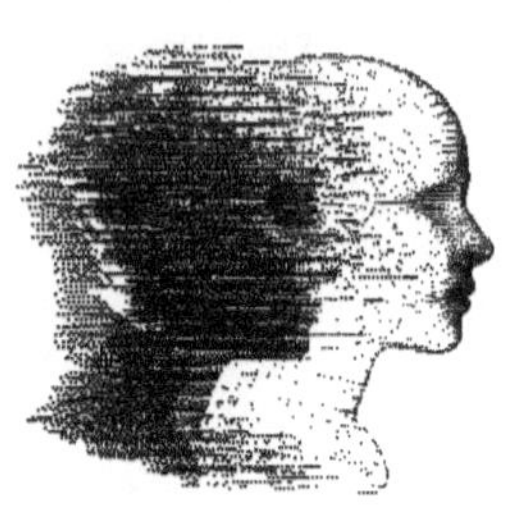

CHAPTER 24

Just seven hours after Vince wired the retainer to Sherlock Sleuths he got an email from Clatch with another jpeg file attached. In his email, Clatch said, "Vince, here's another photo I'd like you to look at. Look carefully and then call me."

Vince opened the jpeg. It was another picture of Garrison. It was a younger Garrison with a giant surprise around his neck—a priest's clerical collar. *Give me a freakin break. I knew he was a bastard-bastard, but a priest? I cannot believe this*, he thought, as he dialed Clatch's cell phone.

"Hello, Vince. I thought the photo I just sent would get your attention. What do you think?"

"Whadda I think! Are you kidding me? I do not fucking believe it—Garrison Venable is a Jesus freak and my sister never knew it! I only knew him a few days, but he didn't seem religious or creepy that way to me. What happened?

Did they kick him out for doodling little altar boys? Where'd you get the picture?"

Clatch took his time. After a few seconds' pause, he said, "Vince, you studied the picture, right? It's Garrison but with a clerical collar, right? That's what you think, right?"

"What are ya saying, Clatch? That Garrison's not a priest—the photo is fake—he just stole a clerical collar and pretends to be a priest?"

"No, the guy in the picture is a priest. There's no doubt of that. But this picture is not *Garrison* Venable. This picture is of *Gilbert* Venable. Do you know about Father Gilbert Venable?"

"Shut up, man! Gilbert Venable is a guy who looks exactly like Garrison Venable and he's a priest? This ain't some weird Halloween joke?"

"It's real. Father Gilbert Venable is a priest in a dirt monastery just outside of Hobbs, New Mexico. He's there today—I mean he's actually there in Hobbs. We have an agent in Las Cruces; he's a good man. His name is Manny Gutierrez. He drove to Hobbs last night when I called him in on the case. He knocked on the church door about twenty minutes ago. An older priest pointed to an Adobe house in back of the little church. Manny knocked on that door and actually talked to Father Gilbert, in person and . . ."

"Hey, man this is fucked. Totally. I don't know how this could be. Garrison is in Hobbs under a different name. He's calling himself Gilbert and hiding in a church? That's what you're saying . . ."

"Vince, you need to slow down. Listen to me. Father Gilbert Venable is Garrison Venable's twin brother. We have a two-page dossier on him. I'll send it to you. We have other pictures as well. And, we are building a longer dossier on your man—Garrison, the identical twin. We have his education record, his clinical licenses in Australia, and several things he wrote while in Ohio. They are twins, but we have no pictures of them together, or any mention in the public records of either of them about being a twin. This could help us find Garrison. I've instructed the Las Cruces associate to back off. We don't want to spook Father Gilbert."

"Why the hell not? Maybe he's in on the fraud. Maybe he's hiding Garrison there in Las Cruces?"

"No, Vince. Our agent, Manny Gutierrez, is in Las Cruces. Father Gilbert is in Hobbs. We are putting a team on him, and we'll watch him from a distance."

"Can you tap his phone?"

"No, not without a warrant. I mean we have the technical capability to do it, but it's too risky. There are other ways to find out whether the brothers are in touch. Leave that part to us. Did you know that identical twins share the same DNA? We're arranging for our Phoenix office to come to your rental house in Phoenix and do some swabbing. That way we can get Garrison's DNA profile without getting his blood. That may be helpful in our search. And we have other photos of Gilbert, the priest, without his clerical collar. We only have a few of Garrison, but I've studied both. They are mirror images of one another."

"What are we waiting for, if your man's got him in sight?"

"We'll talk to him soon. But I want a deep interview of Father Gilbert. He can tell us background things that will help us figure Garrison out, and maybe where he might be hiding. What we know as adolescents and as young adults often frames our thinking about what to do in times of stress. Garrison will know about that because of his psychology degree. Start sending me emails with other things you know about Garrison. We have five people looking now, and we're adding New Mexico and Texas to the geographical search map. Any questions, Vince?"

Vince was too bewildered to question Clatch. But he started making a list now that he knew the bastard-bastard had a freakin' twin.

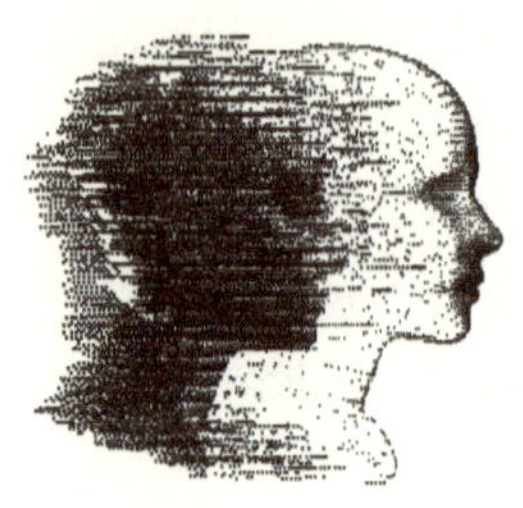

CHAPTER 25

Vince was beside himself thinking about how crazy the twin thing was with Garrison. He was bouncing around the Open Network using different browsers to learn about twin psychology. He thought that if identical twins have the same DNA, then maybe they shared mental disorders too. *You know,* he thought, *the multiplicity thing— dissociative identity disorder is a mental disorder, right? So maybe Garrison and Gilbert have it.* He googled that and found a study done in Minnesota about identical twins who didn't grow up in the same family and didn't know they had a twin until they were in their twenties. The study found a whole bunch of similarities. What fascinated him was that the ones in the study were virtual strangers but were bound by blood and genetics. Some shrinks figure genes are at the core of personality.

Given Vince's own status as an alter, he had a different take on the identical twin thing. He leaned toward the possibility that twins are similar to alters of one another. Crazy as it was, he just couldn't shed it completely. Was Garrison like an alter of Gilbert? Or was it the other way around? Which one was the dominant personality state? Since some DID people had multiple alters, were Garrison and Gilbert alters of a born person, is that what we got here?

Vince found an old research paper written in June 1998 that had so many technical terms he got almost nothing from it. The title was troubling—*Twin Study of Dissociative Experience.* So, twins are like the rest of us? Is that it? The abstract was scientific mumbo-jumbo, but had hints. He'd been used to hints all his life. Hints about Vivian, and how much she knew about him. He long ago accepted that he was she and she was he, sort of. Having dissociative experiences at separate times was his existence. She took time out when she got really scared. He'd show up to help. *But here's the bad part*, he thought. *Every time I help her, it means I'm timed out and she comes back.* He could forget about Garrison and Gilbert once they caught Garrison and got the money he stole back. But then what? He made notes about the study.

Twin study—relative influence of genetic and environmental measures—two measures of dissociative capacity identified—pathological and nonpathological dissociative experiences—suggested common genetic factors—cognitive dysregulation, affective lability, and suspiciousness—particular aspects of personality disorder also influence dissociative capacity.

What did that mean? He leaned forward, put his arms across on the desk, and rested his forehead on his hands. *WTF does this mean!* He was getting mad at himself for being so stupid when the house phone rang. At first he looked at his iPhone, and then realized it was the mobile phone connected to the Cox house alarm system. There was a handset in almost every room in the house. This was the first time he'd heard it ring since he got here.

He clicked on the answer button but said nothing. A few seconds went by. He heard a coughing sound, followed by a wheezing intake of breath.

"Hello," he said tentatively.

"Yes. Hello. I am Lars. Who is answering this phone? I am calling Mr. Garrison."

Vince asked, "Who are you and how did you get this number?"

"I am Lars. Lars Gustaffson. Mr. Garrison is accounting person working for Emergence Incorporated. Yes?"

Vince relaxed, "Yes, but this is not his number. How did you get this number?"

Sounding irritated, the caller increased his volume.

"I get number from real estate person name of Ida. I get her name from Zillow website, looking up address Mr. Garrison told me to write down. Maybe to send priority mail if my email does not work."

"Ida, you say? My name is Vince. I work for Emergence Incorporated. Ida is the rental agent on this house—how did you get the telephone number?"

"I already told you. From Zillow! When Mr. Garrison does not answer phone, does not send email, I get worried.

So I type street address on Zillow and it tells me call real estate agent. I call. Ida tells me telephone number. Now I find you. You answer phone number. So tell me, Mr. Vince, what is happening with our family trust agreement? You confirmed our wire transfer. But then nothing. Are you related to Vinessa?"

Vince sat back down in his computer chair.

"All right, Mr. Gustaffson, now I understand. Garrison has a mild case of COVID, but is getting better. He was in the hospital and is now quarantined and taking oxygen every day. We hope he is back at work in two or three weeks."

"Good to hear that. But now question again. What is happening with our family trust agreement?"

"Yes, I can understand now. Please do not worry. Vinessa is not here right now, but . . ."

"We know that already. She is in Victoria at *The Empress*. My Valentina talked to her once already. So there is no problem—you're saying that?"

"Yes, exactly. I'm saying that. This pandemic is slowing all financial transactions down, but it's just a delay. You will be getting a dividend in three months. Remind me how much you sent to Garrison for trust placement."

The line went quiet for a minute. Vince waited. He could hear the wheezing on the line and knew the caller was thinking about what to say.

"Well, if you're working for him, you can look at record and my bank wire transfer to Mr. Garrison. But maybe he has his laptop with him at hospital? Is that so?"

"Yes, sir, that's part of it. Of course all families' data is backed up to other servers in the cloud. You know about that, right? The thing is I can't access the backup files right now because our Internet signal down here is down again. Does that happen where you are?"

"Well, sometimes, but Canada has big bandwidth. Not worry about that. I tell you now. We wired three hundred forty-five thousand dollars Canadian to Mr. Garrison. I made notes. He told me that would be two hundred sixty-eight thousand dollars US. I forget currency exchange rate that day. You have money safe, right? Even if Mr. Garrison die of COVID, our money is safe. That is right?"

"Yes, sir, that is right. But now that I've got you on the phone, could I ask you a small administrative favor? I'm checking the wire instructions we're sending to Canadian families. Could you send me a copy of the wire transfer instructions that Mr. Garrison sent to you—you know, with the name, account number, and ABA routing number on it? That would help me while we're waiting for Mr. Garrison to come back."

"Yes. OK. Small favor I do for you. Give me email address down there in Arizona. We might come there some day. Canadians love Arizona in the springtime. Baseball and golf, right?"

"Yes, sir. Thanks a lot. I'll wait for your email."

Garrison didn't have long to wait. The promised email came in ten minutes later. Garrison's wiring instructions to the International Bank and Trust were vital. Now he knew where that bastard-bastard must have started the chain of transfers he used to steal the family trust funds. He'd send a copy to Clatch to start the search. *We're gonna get you, shithead!*

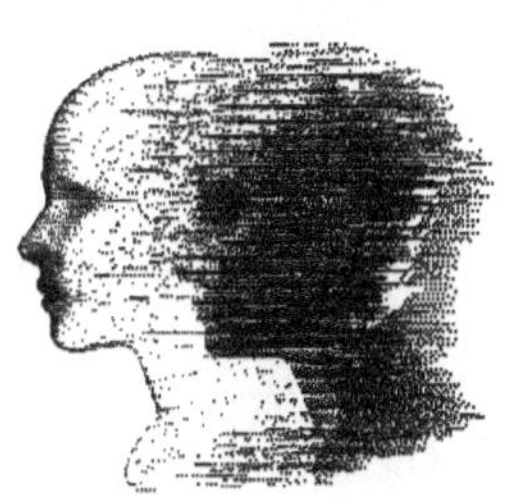

CHAPTER 26

Garrison reached the outskirts of Houston two days later. His Trek odometer insisted he'd driven 1,176 miles. He muttered to himself, which was becoming a habit, *Seems like five thousand freakin' miles.* Over the last nine days, he'd become obsessive about miles, rest stops, fast food, out-of-the-way grocery stores, Coors Lite, and Irish whiskey. The Google Maps app was getting more attention than his basic get-outta-Phoenix plan. Checking it for the nine-thousandth time, he learned that Key West was 1,345 miles due east. *Ain't that the shits*, he muttered, *I'm only half way. Who 'n hell wrote this plan anyway!*

He decided to stay on I-10, cross the sprawling metro area, and get across to the northeast side. Google implied that Jacinto City might be a good place to pull in and take his hands off the steering wheel—he was beginning to hate steering wheels. Wikipedia told him Jacinto City was "part of the Houston–Sugar Land–Baytown metropolitan area and is bordered by the cities of Houston and Galena Park. The population was 10,553 at the 2010 census." Like always, he was irritated at Madame Wiki's sloppy use of language—like "part of." *What does she mean? Part of? It's either in or out, right. A city can't be part of another city, can it?*

OK, so Houston didn't want it. It's a "bedroom community for local industry." As he drove into it, he could see industry all around. Huge cranes. Thousands of enormous tanks. Oil booms. Factories. Giant chimneys spewing smoke. But also big swatches of green, with trails and bikes and a few people. Seemed un-busy, not like central Phoenix. He pulled over at a Chevron with a Wendy's next door. He got gas, parked at Wendy's, put his mask on, and got takeout. Eating at his little dining table inside the Trek, he surfed the area for a KOA campground. The San Jacinto Riverfront RV Park was not too far off. The satellite view showed water. He couldn't quite tell whether it was the Gulf of Mexico, but it was definitely water. It got him thinking about Key West and the water down there.

A half hour later, he eased the Trek into a double space for just $75 a night. It had it all for a guy on the lam, he thought. Pull-thru sites. Electric 50 AMP. Restrooms. Showers. Pool. Hot tub. Wi-Fi. A store with RV supplies and snacks. Peaceful surroundings even though he could hear the interstate at night. View of the water was nice, but it wasn't the Gulf. Maybe a bayou.

On the second day, he lost the open space next to him. A woman wearing a Dallas Cowboys baseball hat pulled in driving a new white F-250 pulling a fifth-wheel luxury no-doubt-about-it thirty-footer. It had four pullout slides, probably slept six, he thought, and sold new for well over a hundred grand. He watched her as she got out and started the set-up with the electricity hook-up, water, and wheel blocking. *Where's her husband?* he thought. He'd find out the next day when she knocked on his door before he fixed breakfast.

"Mornin', ya'll," she said with a smile, extending the drawl. His first guess at her age was maybe forty, but it was hard to tell because she was masked, pony-tailed, and wearing a black sweatshirt over jeans. She wore boots, had brilliant-white teeth, and what some would call a "February" face. She was either worried or depressed, maybe both, he sensed, feeling a mental-health diagnosis coming on.

"Good morning."

"Hate to bother ya'll, but my Wi-Fi connection won't connect. Do you or maybe your wife know anything about hook ups? I called the office and walked over but there's no one inside."

"Well, miss," he said lamely, "I don't have a wife but I came in two days ago and mine hooked up pretty easy. I'd be willing to take a look at yours if you want."

"Fine and dandy. I'm Sharon and you are . . ."

"Miller. Just let me turn the stove down and I'll be over."

She walked in front of him. He liked her from behind too. It turned out that her Wi-Fi hook-up problem was an easy fix. She had a Dell XPS laptop, running Windows 10 with a touchscreen. He used the settings tab to get to the Internet connections and saw she was trying to connect to some other RV, probably parked nearby, rather than the San Jacinto Riverfront network. Once that was fixed, she was online.

"That's so sweet of you," she said. Now that they were inside her unit, she took off her mask and her sweatshirt. She wore a Trump MAGA T-shirt and he changed his mind about her age. Thirty-seven tops, he thought, given her figure—maybe a pop-up bra. What really caught his attention was the tattoo on her left forearm running down from her elbow to the top of her hand. It was a double helix line, very thin, almost delicate, and red and blue intertwined around her arm and wrist, topping out on her hand with a small red flower. It had that $500 look, even though it was faint.

"Have you eaten, yet?" she asked.

"No, I was just starting to fry a slice of Spam and top it off with a smashed egg."

"Do you mind if I ask your age? I don't mean to be personal, but as a single woman and a recent divorcee, I always wonder."

"I'm twenty-nine going on nineteen."

She smiled. "Well, I celebrated my fortieth on the courthouse steps when my ex and me exchanged good-bye vows. We vowed never to see one another again, after our disastrous four-year marriage. He got the house and the boat and I got the truck and this not-too-shabby fifth wheel. I hate the idea you're eating something as grim as Spam. I cook a mean jalapeno chili omelet, with sweet onions. My ex was a meat-eater, like you, but I'm an eyelash vegetarian. Do you know that term?"

"No."

"I don't eat anything that has eyelashes. Fish and plants—that's me! Could I thank you by sharing my omelet, and maybe a tequila sunrise to start the day?"

That's how it started. Goddamn good omelet.

Over the omelet, which was too hot for him, and a half-and-half tequila and OJ over store-bought ice, they traded recent backgrounds. His was mostly fake, and he could not quite place her in his therapy-driven mindset. She talked openly about how happy she was to be rid of her ex, but the look on her face made that doubtful.

"Well, Sharon, I'm glad to know you're a happy divorcee, but still, how do you really feel about it?"

"Really, that's your question? What are you? A traveling shrink in a classic hard-shell motor home?"

"No, sorry for putting it that way. I'm not a psychiatrist. I'm a nurse practitioner and have been a therapist for the last four years. Most people are depressed right after a divorce, even if they did get the truck and the most beautiful fifth trailer I've ever seen. By the way, I didn't get your last name."

"Didn't give my last name. Do last names matter in RV parks? I mean, the thing is I'm thinking on whether to change my last name on account of the divorce. My name's on the door of the facility we built together, so I might keep it for business purposes. On the other finger, so to speak, I hate the bastard now, so I'm thinking on reverting to my maiden name. That's quaint, don't you think—having *maiden* names?

"Guess not," he said, wondering what 'n hell she meant by that.

"So, Miller, is that how you thank me for cooking breakfast—free therapy?"

"Sure, if you need some. Adjusting to life after a divorce takes time. The faithful spouse feels worse than the cheating one. It's milder than post-traumatic stress disorder. You don't have that—your easy smile and deftness with a frying pan disprove that. And you're not clinically depressed, I'm pretty sure of that."

"Well, Miller, I'm glad to know you. I had a fling five years ago with a man from New Mexico. His last name was Miller. Is that your last name or your first?

"Hell if I know for sure. You see, my folks were not exactly married. My brother and me just called them Mom and Dad. Now my brother, he went by Gilbert. We were sort of farmed out in grade school to an old-maid aunt when Mom and Dad split up."

"But what was your last name?"

"It's a secret, known only to Gilbert and me. And the three-room school in New Mexico. Most everyone there went by first name only—but it started with a 'V.' I could tell you, but then I'd have to swear you to secrecy, the New Mexico way. You know about that, right?

"Can't say I do."

"Well, we'd have to make a little cut on our pinkie fingers, and then mix the blood on our foreheads. You up for that?"

"Hell no. You stay Miller and I'll stay Sharon. Now what makes you sure I don't have PTSD?"

"Sharon," he answered after taking a half-minute to gather his own defenses, "PTSD is clinical depression. Post-divorce blues fall into simpler and easier to treat situations. It's called adjustment disorder or situational depression."

"How long are you staying here in the industrial part of Galveston Bay?"

"Don't know, Sharon. To tell you the truth, I'm sort of running away from a bad job, and my Trek has always been good medicine for me. I'm from Idaho and on my way to New Orleans. I just stop wherever the mood takes me."

"So you might be parked next door for the next day or two?"
"Yeah," he said, nodding and drawing the word out, hoping it sounded tentative.

"Well, here's an idea. I'm here to commiserate with my sister-in-law who lives in Baytown. It's a short drive from here. She's a boxer, like me. Actually, we trained together before she gave it up and became a paralegal for a collections lawyer. She's married to him now and says it's fun tracking down bail bond jumpers. How about I cook breakfast for us tomorrow and the next day? Three days of post-divorce therapy in exchange for three days of not eating Spam for breakfast."

"What's your sister-in-law's husband's name? I ask only because I might be needing a collections lawyer soon. A dude in El Paso owes me some money, and I might have to sue him."

"His name is Ernesto Quintana. My sister-in-law's name is Priscilla Quintana-Baca. We call her QB for short."
"We?"

"Yeah, we. See, her husband is my brother. The family called me SQ and him EQ. It's a stupid family thing."

"So, should I call you Sharon or SQ?"

"You're not saying it right. If you were a TexMex like me you'd roll it off your tongue like *Ess Cue*."

"So you're Spanish, right?"

"No, I'm Mexican. And I'm Texan too. Across our border on the west, you have New Mexico. They are snotty and think they are new. Where I grew up in West Texas, we were always more old Mexico than old Spanish."

"Well, we have something in common. My brother lives in Hobbs, New Mexico. I've never been there but I know it's very close to the West Texas border."

"Get outta town! Hey, man, you're talking to a girl who was born in Seminole, Texas! It's the next watering hole due west of Hobbs. Just thirty-one miles away. *Que no?*"

"I've never been to either watering hole. My asshole twin brother lives in Hobbs."

Once the words slipped out of his mouth he regretted them. He had no business telling someone he'd met thirty minutes ago anything about him, or his family. He tried humor to lighten the moment.

"But hey, we're Irish. So when we were born, my dad insisted on knowing who the other man was."

Sharon looked puzzled, "Other man? What other man?"

"Sorry, I forgot. You're Mexican, not Irish. And by the way my last name is Miller. My first is Lee and my middle name is Stanna. Miller is an Irish name meaning 'grain-grinder.' It comes from men who made their living grinding grain at a mill. Seems fitting for me. My whole life has been a grind one way or the other. My twin brother grinds confessions; he's a priest."

She fixed them another tequila sunrise and they moved from the breakfast booth to the two facing arm chairs that swiveled back from the circular front window.

Picking up on the post-divorce therapy talk, he said, "So, you got the fifty cay truck, the one-hundred cay fifth wheel, and alimony to boot, right? What do you need me for? You got money and you're rid of him, right?"

"I got my half of our business we built together. It wasn't a gift from the nice judge. He ran the weight lifting, fitness training side. I ran the women's martial arts side. But I'm mad as hell at him. He was a cheater, and I never did."

"Infidelity is a deep emotional wound," he said, wishing he'd said no, thanked her for breakfast, and trekked on down the road. He had no business risking anything by talking a stranger out of her post-divorce funk.

"Was that part of you counseling practice—divorce caused by infidelity, leading to situational depression—isn't that what you called my situation?"

"Yes, well, every mental health therapist gets some post-divorce patients. America is awash in infidelity and depression. Both need understanding, time, and sometimes a few therapy sessions. Your deal is you cook and I ask questions tomorrow and Friday, right?"

"Yeah, that sounds about right. I mean, I don't hate the guy, I just resent the fact that he kept on lying about it. If he'd come out and admitted it, maybe we'd still be together. But lying on top of cheating is too much for a West Texas girl to take; know what I mean?"

"West Texas? Is it that different from the rest of Texas? What do you mean when you say it's too much for a West Texas girl to take?"

"They say you know a girl from West Texas when her mother is the one who gets in a fist fight after the kid loses a sporting event. My mother was one of the first female boxers back in the seventies. We moved to Midland from Seminole and she worked hard to get into fistfights. Know what I mean?"

Garrison had no idea what she meant, so he returned to form. Mental health counselors treat mostly by asking questions, knowing that the best therapeutic outcomes come from self-understanding.

"Did you get into boxing because your mother encouraged it?"

"No, I just liked hitting people."

"I only asked because infidelity is very complex, and if you're the innocent party there's always a desire to fight back. Sometimes that gets physical. Did that happen in your case?"

"Do you mean did I slug her? No, I didn't. But now that it's over, I wish I had."

"So, you felt hostile toward her, not him? Is that what you're feeling now?"

"No, Mr. Counselor, I mean I wished I'd gone physical, not just sitting home and crying about it. In West Texas we fight for our men, and I never did. I just let her take him away. That's what pisses me off the most."

"If you had fought her for him, thinking back on it, would it have mattered? You know there's a good deal of research into the *why* questions. I could earn that great breakfast you just cooked by asking the usual questions. Why did this happen? Why didn't you know earlier? Was it him or her that started it? Who opened the door? What could you have done to keep her from just waltzing through the door and out with your husband?"

"Oh for Christ's sake, Miller, is it that simple? He told the mediator in front of me that he found what he called 'satisfaction' across town because he felt a lack of intimacy at home. After our first two years, we had sex four or five times every year and then got divorced. Isn't that enough? What do you men want sex for in the first place? What was I supposed to do, anyway? I wanted celibacy, and he wanted anal sex."

"Celibacy? Really? That's a condition I know a lot about."

Sharon got up and cleared the dishes. Over her shoulder, she asked, "Miller, are you celibate?"

"My brother is. We're fraternal twins; he's a Catholic priest."

Even the most expensive RVs like this one, with both slides out, were like living in a hallway. Suddenly, Garrison felt trapped. *What the fuck did I say that for?* he thought, cursing himself. It was embarrassing. He sensed his breathing was rushed and she could see him trembling, even though her back was turned. He felt locked in the swivel chair with his back to the steering wheel and her five feet away, smiling at him.

"Well good goddamn, you had me there for a minute. Your brother is in Hobbs, right? I thought fraternal twins were inseparable."

He felt his heart rate returning to normal.

"No, that's the odd thing. I mean we grew up wearing matching clothes and playing tricks on adults by pretending we were the other twin, not the one who knocked over the display stand or threw the rock over the backyard fence. But we lived in two different states. When we became teenagers, he went away to a seminary, and I went to public high school. Then our folks split up and we never spent any time together. I'm not celibate."

"Well, that's a relief," she said, as he slid out of the big swivel armchair.

"Thanks for the chili omelet," he said, as he stepped down to the concrete pad.

"Same time tomorrow morning?" she said to his back. He waved his hand in the air.

A half hour later, she pulled the big Ford rig out from under the fifth wheel and drove to Baytown. When she got back at almost 10 p.m., after a late dinner with her sister-in-law, she was not surprised to see his space was empty. As she got into bed after double locking the door, she couldn't help feeling sorry for the poor bastard. *Jesus,* she thought, *maybe he really was celibate. He got his religious vows, but without the clerical collar.*

Later, she would have trouble explaining why she called the RV park's front office. But on the spur of the moment, she tapped in the office number she'd used to make her reservation.

"This Jean, front office manager."

"Hi Jean, this is Sharon. I'm in space 29A. Can ya'll do me a small favor? See, I met the nice man in 29B yesterday and he left this morning. I need to thank him for his help. Do you have his cell number—he said he'd called in for his reservation, just like I did. His name was Miller."

Jean gave her the cell number from the registration form on her computer.

CHAPTER 27

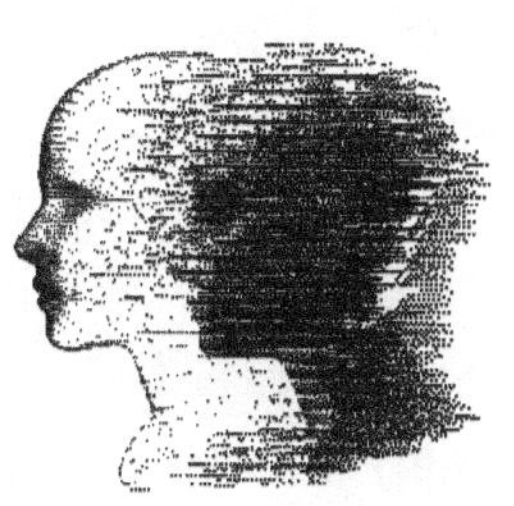

As they had agreed, Clatch sent Vince a status email every morning. And as Vince insisted, they talked on the phone at precisely 6 p.m. every night, Mountain Standard Time. The morning email had identified the status of the four ongoing search efforts. First, there were no police records identifying Garrison Venable. Second, the background checks revealed academics, jobs, apartment rentals, driver's licenses, one automobile purchase, and very little participation in social media. Third, no surveillance operation was in process because none of the sub-agents had any idea where he was. Fourth, Clatch had a new recommendation.

"So, Clatch," Vince asked when he took the call, "you have a new idea, right?"

"Yes, it's based on three days of not getting a track on your man. We've talked about it and think you should consider a sizable reward for anyone who identifies him and leads to his capture."

"Whoa there, Clatch. I told you we don't want the police involved. You're not talking about one of those 'Silent Witness' programs are you? Where someone gives up the secret location of the bank robber and the cops get their man. We can't do that."

"No, Vince, I'm thinking about the much more common reality. Bail jumping. There are bail bond dealers all over America who try to find bail jumpers. I'm thinking we should post a private reward for information on Garrison Venable. By private I mean it's only available to people who are incentivized to find him for us. Ordinary people. Offer a large sum, say ten thousand dollars, and we can engage every skip tracer in the country."

"But he must be avoiding us by using fake ID cards, not using credit cards, and not taking public transportation. That's what you've been telling me, right? We don't have anything, do we?"

"Garrison, we have two things. We have his picture. We have his twin brother's picture. And we'll have his DNA, because we will dig it out of the rental house where he lived. You said he lived in the casita there, right? He could not have cleaned it well enough to avoid our team. Are they finished yet?"

"Yes, the two guys in PPE you sent were in the casita all day. They left about an hour ago, after trashing it."

"All right, we'll have to wait maybe a week or two for results. In the meantime, we have his picture. We'll distribute that to maybe a hundred collection agencies and skip tracers.

We'll tell them this is a private reward. Just find the guy and let us know. No capture. No publicity. But you get ten cay if you give us his current location and we catch him."

"Clatch, that's another thing. Even if we find him, we cannot involve the police. The people who he embezzled from won't come forward. Your people don't have the right to arrest him, do they?"

"No, they don't. But you have the right to interrogate him yourself. You're representing the victims of what you think is a giant Ponzi scheme. That's what you called it, right? A Ponzi scheme? We have sources who, for a large fee, can detain him for a few hours. You can interrogate him by Zoom. If you threaten him with prosecution, maybe he will tell you what you really need—the names and wiring instructions of the bank chain he probably used to hide what he stole. Once you have that, you might be able to reverse the transactions and move the money back into your company's control. Emergence Incorporated gets its money back. Then, my people let him go. What's he going to do, sue them for wrongful arrest? He's a thief and could never make a civil claim like that work in court. He'd be inviting public prosecution, even if your people won't help by cooperating with state or federal fraud agents. What do you think about this idea?"

What Vince thought and what he would tell Clatch were miles apart. He told Clatch he loved the idea but ten grand was too low. Raise it to twenty-five grand, he said. That's enough to make people sit up and pay attention to every RV on the road. And we should ask no questions—just pay the reward to the person who leads us to the bastard-bastard.

Vince said he'd interrogate Garrison but it wouldn't be by Zoom. What he didn't tell Clatch was his last step. Garrison would get the same red-duct-tape treatment he'd given Julia Baby in Houston. Then he'd dump Garrison in the Galveston Bay in a fifty-five-gallon drum of fluoroantimonic acid.

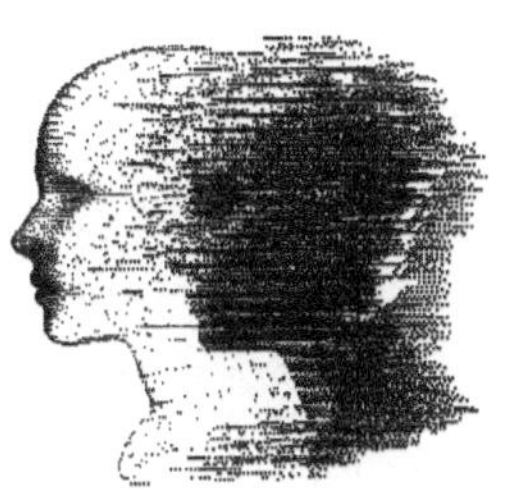

CHAPTER 28

While Garrison was driving the Trek southeast to the Arkansas border, Sharon drove her fifth wheel as far south as you can go in Texas. She took I-45 for the fifty-six mile drive down to Galveston Island. She had a dozen choices but picked the Sand Piper RV Resort because it was on the Gulf, had an infinity pool, and was walking distance from the best hotels and restaurants on the long strip island. She got a premium spot for $70 per night. Once she was parked and hooked up to electricity, propane, Wi-Fi, and cell coverage, she called her sister-in-law, QB, in Bayside.

"Sharon, you rich bitch, where are you now, trucking on down the road somewhere looking for a place to spend your money?"

"Not hardly, cue-bee. I've got a fancy truck, a fifth-wheel trailer home, and four thousand three hundred dollars a month in alimony. That's not rich in Houston and damn sure not rich on Galveston Island."

"So, is that Miller guy from the San Jacinto RV Park gonna work out for you? He sounded kind of cute."

"Nah, he skipped out after just one jalapeno breakfast. Guess he didn't like my cooking."

"Well, sis-in-law, reason I'm asking is on account of Miller being a common name. You sure that's his real name? "

"I think he's Irish," Sharon interrupted.

"What's his last name?"

"Why are you asking? He's so yesterday, like everything else in my life."

"Just humor me, Sharon; it wasn't Gilbert was it?"

"No, he told me some bullshit story about him and his brother. He said his brother's name was Gilbert. "

"Well, SQ, hold on to your seat belt, girl. There a state-wide search going on for a man named Garrison who might be traveling with his brother, named Gilbert. There's a big reward for anyone who knows where they are! Seems like Gilbert and Garrison are identical twins and look exactly alike. There's a photo of one of them on the reward poster."

"Reward? I know you guys are in the collection business—oh, sorry, you call it the recovery business. Is this a wanted criminal thing, you know like a serial killer with a chain saw?

"No, it's not even criminal. It's private, not involving law enforcement. We see it every once in a while—a private reward is circulated among recovery lawyers like Ernie, bail bond offices, and skip tracers. It usually comes from a high-grade private investigation firm. This one comes from the top one in the country. They call themselves Sherlock

Sleuths. You can check it out at sherlock_sleuths.com. They are a class outfit and usually represent rich families or businesses that need help but don't trust law enforcement. They just posted a big goddamn reward—$50,000. No-questions-asked."

"What does that mean, 'no questions asked'?"

"Well, if it's a criminal case, or if it's a law enforcement agency posting, you get the money only if your information about the person they are looking for is prosecuted on the basis of the information you provided. But if it's a no-questions-asked type thing, then you get the money just for pointing out the missing person to them. Do you remember what the guy you cooked breakfast for looked like?"

"Sure, it's only been a couple days. I'm just not sure about his last name."

"Don't sweat that. I'll email you the reward poster—it's got a head shot of the guy they are looking for. Call me back."

In less than minute her iPad dinged. She flipped open the cover, logged on, went to Outlook, and opened her email. She thought she was gonna pee her jeans. She drummed her boots on the fake wood floor and yelled, *Good Lord a-Mosey! It's him!*

She hit redial on her cell and her sister-in-law picked up on the first ring.

"So is it him?"

"Bet your booty it is! I mean holy shit, what do I do now? Can you and Ernie handle this for me, you know, maybe not give the PI my name right off? What if he's an axe-murderer? I mean Jesus H. Christ. I just had breakfast with him!"

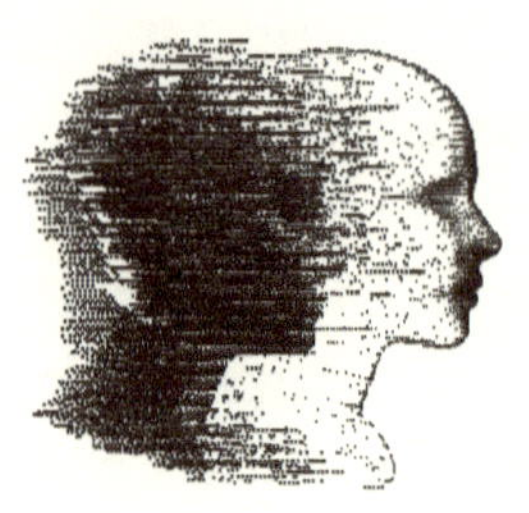

CHAPTER 29

Ernesto Quintana called the number on the reward poster and was put through to an assistant. "Good afternoon," the assistant-sounding voice said, "how may we help you today?"

"You can put me through to the investigator heading the search for Garrison Venable."

"That would be Mr. Clayton Unswor. Who may I say is calling?"

"I'm Ernie Quintana. I'm a lawyer in Baytown."

Seconds later, a stronger voice came on. "This is Clatch, Mr. Quintana. Have you got a bead on Garrison Venable?"

"It's not a bead, Mr. Unswor. My client had breakfast with a man named Miller two days ago. He told her his name was Miller. But he mentioned a brother named Gilbert. But this Miller guy is the spittin' image of the man in your private reward picture I'm looking at. What's the deal here?"

"Call me Clatch, everybody does. Have you done business with us in the past?"

"No, can't say that. I did just look at your website—impressive, I'd say."

"Let me cut to the chase here, Ernie. Our client is a corporation headquartered in Arizona. This is a private matter—no law enforcement involved. They need to find Mr. Garrison Venable as soon as possible. He was last seen traveling with his brother Gilbert. Can your client positively identify the man she knew as Miller and match him to the photo on our reward poster?"

"My client met him day before yesterday, here in Houston. Well, actually Baytown. She just told me a few minutes ago. She can match Miller to the picture. She thought there was something fishy about him keeping his last name a secret—least ways, that's what he told her."

"Well that's close enough in time and place. This is a twenty-five grand reward case and it's yours if we find him on your lead, I mean your client's lead. When can I talk to her?"

"Today, I'm sure. But I'd like a simple email confirming the reward first."

"Can do. My assistant will have it to you immediately. Call me right back when you get it. I'll be waiting for your call."

The email came in two minutes and was obviously a form tailored to this situation. It did the $25,000 dollar job. Ernie called back and this time was put through directly. He gave Clatch the basic information he got from Sharon.

Clatch said he'd catch the next Southwest flight to Houston and hoped he could meet Sharon that evening.

"Is there any chance your client could come to our Houston office this evening? And you are welcome to come along as well."

Their office was in the Embarcadero Center in the heart of downtown Houston. Ernie, Sharon, and Priscilla met Clatch in an oval-shaped conference room on the twenty-ninth floor. After the usual amenities of exchanging business cards and declining anything to drink, Clatch slid an eight-by-ten enlarged photo of the man in the poster across the table to Sharon.

"Ma'am, if you don't mind getting right to it, can you tell me with certainty that the man you met in Baytown day before yesterday is this man?"

"Call me Sharon, everybody does. And yes this is the man. He told me his name was Miller."

"Did he volunteer his name or did you ask him for it?"

"He said his name was Miller. I asked if that was his first name or last. That's when he started dodging and told me he had a brother named Gilbert in New Mexico. But he was the man here in this picture."

"I have many questions, Sharon, but first let me show you another photo."

He pushed the other picture across the table. It was smaller, and in color.

"Is this the same man you had breakfast with?"

"Yes, sure. It's in color but it's him, he might be a year or two younger."

"Well, let me be straight with you, Sharon. The first picture is Garrison Venable. The second picture is his twin brother, Gilbert Venable."

"Oh, yes. He told me he was a twin. By God, they look identical except for one looking a little older."

"You're right. They are twins. They are the same age within a minute or two. The first picture is one taken two years ago when Garrison Venable was in Australia. The second picture is Gilbert Venable, taken in Hobbs, New Mexico, about five years ago. You said he was parked next to your slot. In an RV, I presume. What can you tell me about it?"

"Well, it was old, in good shape, clean, you know. I don't know a lot about RVs or house trailers either."

"But you drive a fifth wheel, pulling a very expensive forty-foot unit. I can barely manage a bumper-pull on our five-foot square motorcycle hauler. That takes some serious experience."

"I grew up driving trucks. We never had a car. I learned how to drive in a one-ton Ford and we had to pull wagons, farm equipment, hay balers. I could back up a flatbed trailer before I got my driver's license. So a fifth wheel is second nature to me."

"Makes sense. Now, what can you tell us about the RV he was driving?"

"Well, it was very boxy. Aluminum siding faded yellow. Big windows, all around. No slide outs—I'd say it was twenty, thirty years old. Big tires, I'd say twenty inches, and square as all hell. Not a curve anywhere. It had a funny name on the front, like track or truck, or no wait. It was Trek. I think it had some kind of desert name on it too, like the Mohave or Painted or something like that."

While she was talking, Clatch's assistant was fingering his iPad.

"Excuse me, Miss. Could it have been Safari?"

"Hell yeah," Sharon said. "That's it, Safari TREK. The trek was in all caps, like a Trump tweet. He's old too."

The assistant passed over his iPad with a picture of a 1994 Safari Trek motor home.

"Oh my God," Sharon screeched. "How the F did you do that?"

The assistant said, "It's the Internet. AI in 4G."

Clatch took over. "So this is the exact vehicle, right? You didn't get the license plate, did you?"

"No, I only saw the front end."

"That's all right. These old jobs are easy to find. New ones are a dime a dozen these days, and harder to find."

"OK, you met a man and he told you his name was Miller. Now we know that man was actually Garrison Venable. What was he wearing, and were his clothes clean or dirty?

"A T-shirt and jeans. But not running shoes, more like loafers. No hat and no belt. That's unusual. Everybody around here wears a belt with a rodeo buckle, whether they earned it or not."

"Anything unusual about his affect? I mean did he seem to sweat, or fidget, or look around while you were talking?"

"No, but now that you ask, he did seem in a little hurry to get inside, like he didn't want to be seen. He wore sunglasses, and of course he had a mask on. Like we all have to do outside, 'cept for Trump people. Once we got in my unit, he took off his mask and his no-see-em sun glasses. He looked like he could use a little sun—he was pale like starchy water."

"Did you have your mask on?"

"Nah, I wear it into stores, but this is Texas you know. We have a right to choose our clothes and our president. I don't like to be told what I can wear but that does not make me want to vote for Trump again. I made that mistake four years ago. And . . ."

Clatch interrupted. "Did Garrison talk about politics? Did he have any logos on that Safari Trek?"

"No, he didn't. No yakaty yak or logos. His T-shirt was grey. He talked very educated, and didn't have an accent, or much of a sense of humor, if you ask me."

"But you felt comfortable with him, right?"

"You know, I did. He seemed like a nice man. And come to think of it, he did have a sense of humor. When I asked him how old he was he said, 'twenty-nine going on nineteen.'"

"When you talked in your upscale motor home, did he mention anything about Australia?"

"No, I don't think so. We talked mostly about my recent divorce."

"Yes, that would make sense. It was just finalized about nine days ago, right? Judge Arellano was sitting, right?"

Ernie stepped in.

"Hey, Clatch. Have you been investigating my client? What the hell is going here?"

"No, Mr. Quintana, we're only investigating Garrison Venable. But I did ask for a quick 'who is she' from my assistant in Dallas. He emailed it and I read it on the taxi ride here from the airport. I happen to know Judge Arellano because she's a very busy divorce court judge. A lot of our cases come out of divorce cases in family court. And before I startle you again, I should mention I know your client is from Seminole, Texas. That is interesting only because the man in the second photo lives in Hobbs, which is only a few miles from Seminole."

Turning back to Sharon, Clatch asked, "I presume you don't know the twin—Gilbert Venable? He was not in Hobbs when you grew up in Seminole. We're not looking for him, but we will be talking to him, hopefully tomorrow. Did Garrison talk about his brother, or just mention his name?"

"It was more a passing reference than a conversation—about the brother. I felt he was uncomfortable talking about family. Actually, I only spent an hour or so with him, and we talked mostly about me, and my situational depression. That's how he described it—situational."

"All right, did you get the sense he was in any way off balance, like scared, or mad, or dangerous?"

"No, see, I only met him because he was parked in the next slot and I couldn't get Wi-Fi to work. He fixed it for me. I offered to cook breakfast. I never would have invited him in had I sensed anything wrong with him. He was clean cut, sounded well educated, and nothing about him bothered me. I told him I was recently divorced, and he mentioned he was a counselor, sort of mental health, you know, and we kidded around for a half hour. When I came back that afternoon, he was gone."

"Were you surprised?"

"Well, yes. A little. We'd kidded about two more breakfasts and two more therapy sessions for me. So yes, it did surprise me a little."

"OK, was there anything you said or asked him about that seemed to upset him or even make him frown?"

Sharon realized there was a lot she didn't know about the man they were after and that bothered her.

"What did he do? I mean you're obviously chasing him for some kind of wrongdoing. Why aren't the police involved, and more importantly, should I be worried about him coming after me if I help you?"

Ernie also chimed in.

"That's right, Clatch. We are not looking for details but your questions suggest the guy was off balance. Do you mean mentally? Does he have a record for anything?"

Clatch was six foot four at least and probably weighed over 230. His hard, square jaw jutted out when he leaned forward at you. He had dark, leathery, wrinkled skin, like a well-polished boot. But his voice was soothing and his manner calm.

"Sorry to worry you, folks. I can't tell you much about our client. But I can say there is no danger here to you, Sharon. This is a financial dispute between my client and the man in that picture. It's about money, not violence. All they want is to find Mr. Venable and get square with him over the financial issue. As you might guess from the size of the reward, a good bit of money is at dispute here. Now anything you can tell me about his demeanor, his mood, his attitude, anything like that?"

Sharon felt slightly foolish so she put on her best smile.

"OK, I'll quit worrying about him and go back to festering on how best to kill my ex. No, there was nothing he said or did . . . well, except for one thing. He told me he was celibate, and I found that remarkable to say to a total stranger."

Clatch nodded his head and asked, "What was the context? I mean were you taking about sexual matters, or something personal?"

"No, now that I think of it, maybe it *was* connected to his brother, a Catholic priest. They are supposed to be celibate, right? They can't get married. And we were talking about my divorce. Nothing personal. I never even mentioned why I got divorced."

They talked for another ten minutes, all the while Clatch kept looking at his watch and the assistant kept pressing keys. As Clatch closed his three-ring binder, he asked, "Is there anything else you know that might help us?"

"Well, maybe. I have his cell phone number."

"God almighty! I forgot to ask you. Lady, I'm certain of two things. We will find Garrison Venable in the next day or two. And when we do it will be because you gave us his vehicle *and* his cell number. You gonna get that twenty-five cay reward."

CHAPTER 30

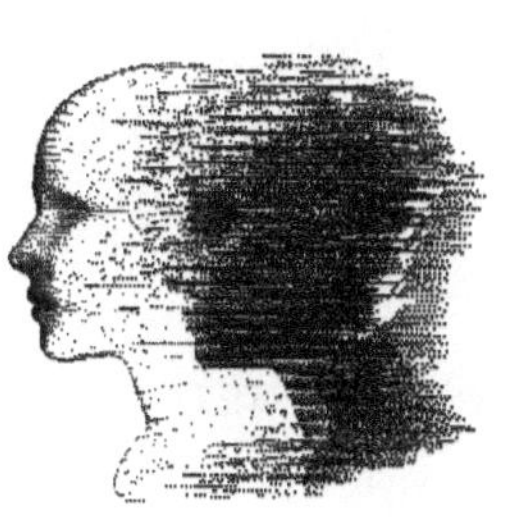

Clatch called Vince in Phoenix the next morning and was surprised to hear a woman's voice when he speed-dialed Vince's iPhone.

"Hello," she said.

"Vince, is this you? Do you have strep or something?"

"I'm sorry. You're calling Vince aren't you? This is his number but he's out. I'm Vinessa. I think you and Vince had some arrangement, but I'm sketchy on what it was."

Clatch was glad he wasn't on a Zoom call or he'd look flushed. *What's this?* he wondered.

"Yes, I was calling Vince. My name's Clatch and I'm calling about a search we have on for an employee of Emergence Incorporated. You're with the company, I'm assuming, right?"

"Yes, I am. I'm the chairwoman. Vince is our CTO. I think I know what you're calling about—it's about Garrison, right?"

"Yes, Miss Vinessa, I . . ."

"Do call me Vinessa, not Miss Vinessa. I'm sure it must sound odd to you, but sometimes Vince gets so involved with one of our projects that he doesn't get around to informing me. Would you be so kind as to bring me up to date, so to speak? I know Garrison's missing and I worry about him. Did Vince ask you to assist us in that?"

"Yes, Vinessa, he did. In fact he signed a substantial retainer agreement with my company. We are a search company, and I'm a private investigator, and . . ."

"Oh, yes, it's coming back now. Sherlock Holmes something, right? You're in Texas. Are you sufficiently funded now? And what can you tell me about Garrison?"

"We have your retainer. Vince arranged a wire retainer. And I have good news for you. We have a very solid lead on Garrison Venable. I think we'll have him close at hand in a few days."

"That would be grand. Where is he?"

"Well, he was in Houston, Texas, just day before last. He's apparently driving cross-country in an old RV, one called a Safari Trek. Does that mean anything to you?"

"No. Garrison has an older car, a Chevrolet, I think."

"Yes, he did, Vinessa. But he sold his 2011 Malibu to a man named Cactus Jack about ten days ago. He bought the Safari Trek in Gilbert, Arizona. That's a suburb of Phoenix right? Our agent in Phoenix had talked to Cactus Jack. He still has the Malibu for sale. We have the VIN on that and the license plate data. And we found the used car dealer in Mesa where Mr. Venable bought the Safari Trek. It is a 1994 model and we have both the VIN number and the license plate, although I doubt it's the one he's using now. I expect we will find the vehicle within the next few days. So, ma'am, should I be reporting back to you, or do you expect Vince to return soon?"

"You may call me at most any time. I don't sleep much when Vince is out. He's my little brother you know, but he comes and goes."

"Right then," Clatch said. "I'll call you at this number. And we need your email address too, if you have one. I'll email you with my contacts, on a going-forward basis."

"Whatever does he think?" Vinessa said under her breath. "He must think I'm a doddering old maid. Pity that."

Thirty minutes later, Clatch got a text. "Clatch, I will arrive Houston International tomorrow night. American Airlines # 722 @ 8:50 CST. Pls book room close to your office. Pls arrange pickup at airport and meeting time your office tomorrow night for update. Find Safari Trek tomorrow? Text back. Vince."

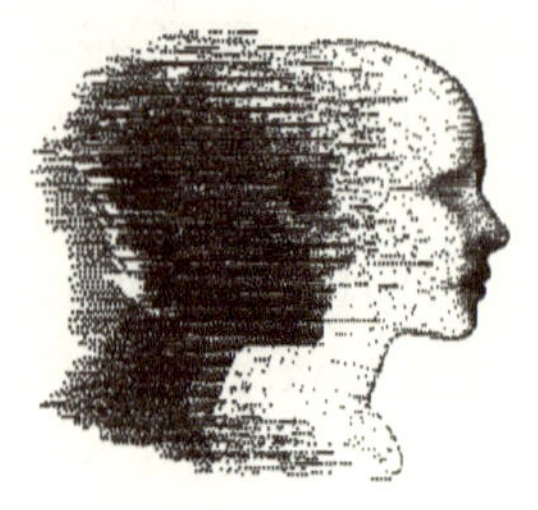

CHAPTER 31

While Vince was in the air, Clatch got a frantic call from their Las Cruces, New Mexico, office. The agent there had been keeping watch on Father Gilbert in Hobbs.

"Clatch here, is this you Manny, you old rascal?"

"Sorry, sir," the caller said in a halting voice. "This is Melanie; I'm the office manager here in Las Cruces. Our agent, Manny Gutierrez, just sent me a text. Apparently he is out of cell service, but can text. I'll read his text for you. 'M. call Clatch in Houston now. Fr. Gilbert Venable gone missing. Will call in maybe one hour. Manny.'"

It took two hours. Manny drove all the way back to the Las Cruces office so he could talk to Clatch over a secure, encrypted phone. He used Signal, via WhatsApp and their encryption protocol for voice and video calls.

"Clatch, hey man, sorry for the delay—I thought this call should be made from the office VOIP rather than my cell phone clicking open cell towers. Here's the thing. The little monastery where Fr. Gilbert lives had a fire of some kind. Scared the hell out of Fr. Gilbert, I guess. Anyway, he told Fr. Raymond, the pastor, he could not stay there. He packed a small bag. He doesn't have a car, so he used Lyft to take him all the way to Carlsbad. From there, he boarded a Greyhound for El Paso."

Clatch asked, "You got a firm track on that?"

"Yeah, I talked to the Lyft driver by phone. He told me he dropped Fr. Gilbert at the Carlsbad bus station. I went there, flashed my creds card, and got the ticket agent to confirm that Fr. Gilbert went to El Paso. They made him produce a photo ID. God, what's this country coming to when you can't even trust a priest when he buys a bus ticket?"

"So, do we have him getting off the bus in El Paso?"

Manny smiled. "No, boss, you don't need an ID to get off. But he didn't get on another bus; we know that. The El Paso agent is Chuko Garcia; you know him, right?"

"Yeah, not that smart, but he does his job. What'd he find out?"

"He confirmed our priest didn't take a bus from there. Nobody saw a man with a white collar around his neck. Everybody in the station was masked. So we're dead stopped there."

"Send Chuko to the train station. Amtrak runs through there."

"Will do, boss. What's your thinking? I'm thinking Amtrak runs west from Union Station in El Paso all the way to Amtrak Station Houston. Maybe Fr. Gilbert is going to wherever his twin is. You had him in Houston day before yesterday. Maybe he called his brother for help, or money, or who knows what. What's the next major city on the rail track between Houston and El Paso?"

"That would be San Antonio. I'll take it from here," Clatch said.

"I'll patch in San Antonio. You work with El Paso. Our man is in an old yellow and tan RV on I-10. His brother is on a train that pretty much follows the I-10. Maybe they are meeting somewhere between Houston and El Paso. Let's check out both ends and see if they meet up in San Antonio."

CHAPTER 32

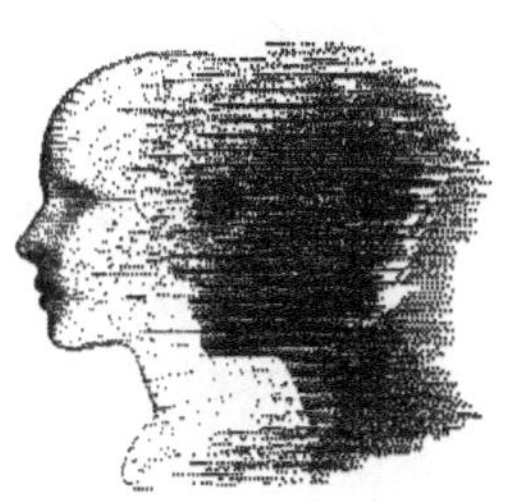

As Garrison drove the Trek out of the San Jacinto Riverfront RV Park two hours after Sharon went to talk to her sister-in-law, he kept muttering to himself, "You fuckin' idiot, she's gonna tell and you're goin' to jail."

He could not remember, even though the conversation was only three hours old, exactly what he'd said about Gilbert. He'd mentioned his name. He'd said something about Hobbs. And he'd told her his brother was a priest. *Way too fuckin' much*, he thought, slamming his palm on the steering wheel. But it had also given him a chance to do something he'd long fantasied. He'd use his twin to make his get-outta-Phoenix plan work.

He pulled over at a truck stop and texted Gil.

"Gil. It's Gare. I'm in big trouble. Need you bad. Come to San Antonio now. Bring your passport. We're going to Santiago. Text me back. No calls."

Back on the freeway, and passing road signs about MAGA, COVID-19, or both, he mentally ticked off ways to turn his blunders with Sharon into positives. A half hour later, he saw a billboard next to the same truck stop where he stopped for gas on the far west side of Houston. It was huge, brightly colored, and nagging. ***"23 and Me!** Use Your DNA To Find Who You Are."*

In the first semester of grad school, he'd gone to a lecture about DNA and twins. He was stunned to discover he and Gil had the same DNA, but different fingerprints. If they took blood from him and from Gilbert and mixed up the vials and names, it wouldn't matter. Their DNA was identical. Any search would reveal he'd sent in that spit vial last year at **23 And Me!**

From that truck stop, Google told him San Antonio was 181 miles due west via I-10. He'd be there in about three hours. He texted Gil. "Gil. It's Gare. I will be in San Antonio in three hours. Where are you? Text back. No calls."

He kept driving for almost an hour when he heard a text message hit his Android. "Am on train to SA. Be there tomorrow morning at 10:30. Where do we meet?"

He texted Gil back. "Meet @ Amtrak Station Parking Lot. Look for old yellow RV with Red Bandanna on Aerial."

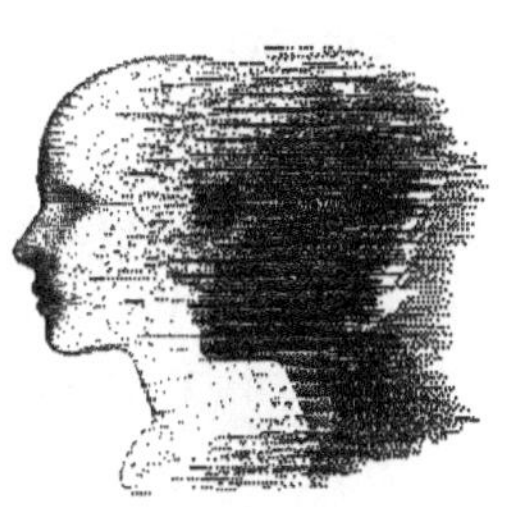

CHAPTER 33

Vince burned up line after line texting back and forth with Clatch on the American Airlines flight from Phoenix to Houston. Clatch infuriated him by refusing to say anything substantive. He just said he'd have a chauffeured car meet him on arrival at Houston International. He arrived almost on time, at 9:20, and jogged down the wide hallway to the lobby. He spotted a short man in a Men's Warehouse black suit wearing black Nikes and a matching driver's cap right out of the 1990s. He held up an iPad that flashed one word: VINCE.

"I'm Vince," he screamed as he jogged toward the short man.

"Let me take your bag, sir. I'm just across the front drive in the chauffers-only parking lane."

Once in the back seat of the Lincoln Navigator, Vince asked, "How long before we reach Clatch's office?"

"About thirty minutes, adjusting for late traffic."

Vince dug a twenty-dollar bill out of his wallet, threw it over the seat to and said, "Make it twenty and you get the twenty."

"Yes, sir," the man said and floored it around a FedEx delivery truck.

When they pulled in, the short man said over his shoulder, "Embarcadero Center, sir. Your meeting is on the twentieth floor. Clatch just texted me. He's waiting for you."

Clatch was waiting as the elevator doors opened on twenty. They shook hands. Vince was surprised by how hard Clatch's hand was. Clatch would have bet on how soft Vince's grip was. Vince didn't say hello.

"Have we got the bastard-bastard yet?"

"Not yet, but we're close."

Clatch took hold of Vince's elbow and nudged him into a large conference room behind a floor-to-ceiling wall of glass.

"That's what you said two days ago," Vince complained.

"Sit down, there's fresh coffee in that pot, but we've got something stronger if you like. Now, Vince, it's good to meet you too. We're closer than we were two days ago. I know there's a lot riding on this, but trust me. We'll have him by this time tomorrow. Here's what we know for sure."

His monologue to his client took five minutes, but all Vince heard was that Garrison was still in the Trek, probably on I-10 headed toward San Antonio and texting messages on his cell phone. He'd used it to send text messages twice in the hour before Vince landed.

"Well, what did the texts say?"

"We don't have the words used, or who he's texting. We only have trace and trap records from AT&T that identify the location of cell towers he's clicking on. That's why we think he's on I-10 headed for the Alamo. Maybe that's his last stand."

"Trap and trace? What 'n hell's that?"

Clatch pointed to his assistant and said, "Explain it, will you?"

The assistant smiled at Vince. "A trap and trace device or process can capture incoming electronic or other impulses. It's technical, but basically they identify the originating number or other routing and addressing. But we don't get the text or words spoken."

"How'd we get the bastard-bastard's cell phone number?"

"From Sharon. She also gave us the make and model of the RV he's driving while texting. Our man in Phoenix got the VIN number from the seller."

"Who 'n hell is Sharon?"

"A forty-something gal that took a short fancy to Garrison, but is now helping us. She wants the reward money you authorized us to pay."

"Do we trust her?"

"Here's a copy of the summary of what she told us yesterday. You'll see she was pretty observant. Her recollections have turned out to be spot-on accurate."

"What about the brother—the priest, or Rabbi, or whatever he is?"

Clatch slid another stapled report across the table.

"Here is what we know about Fr. Gilbert. Near the end, you'll see we think he's on a train on his way to San Antonio, now."

Vince glared at Clatch. "Then if you think the bastard-bastard is driving to San Antonio and his brother is on a train to San Antonio, why n' fuck are we sitting here in Houston?"

"Vince, we're sitting here because your man was here while you were flying here from Arizona. I have a Lear Jet on stand-by status. San Antone's a thirty-four minute flight from here. Once we get confirmation that he's there, we'll go get him. Meanwhile, you should check into your hotel. It's just across the street. Cindy will show you to the lobby. I'm there too, but I'll stay here where we have good coms and status reports. We've got men and women working there to spot either the yellow RV, or a priest looking for the same vehicle. They are identical twins, you know; so if we find one, we'll find the other."

CHAPTER 34

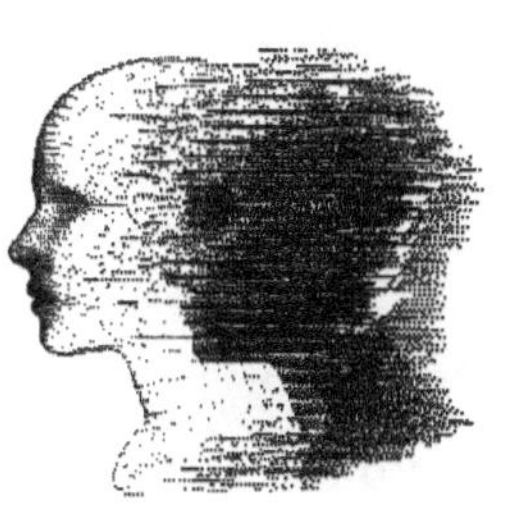

Garrison arrived at the outskirts of San Antonio six hours ahead of his brother. He'd been using Xanax on and off for five years and knew well its usefulness in reducing anxiety and calming his on-fire brain. He didn't know whether it could be a knockout drug.

He pulled into the Petro Shopping Center, filled up, and parked in front of a nearby Subway. He masked up, went inside, and ordered two foot-long salami sandwiches with mayo and pickles, no lettuce, two bags of chips, and a thirty-two-ounce loyalty cup of Simply Lemonade. Back in the Trek, he laid out a map and a note pad, and googled benzodiazepines. One researcher, from a mid-level university in a Southern state, answered his question.

Knockout drugs include alcohol and liquid ecstasy. The most important are benzodiazepines. Within ten minutes, victims report disturbed perception, a

dazed feeling, disinhibition, and lack of willpower.
Knockout drugs are difficult to detect because they
are rapidly metabolized and can only be detected
in the blood for a maximum of twenty-four hours.

He had no way to acquire liquid ecstasy, but he had a dozen or more Xanax tabs in his canvas gym bag. With the basics down pat, Garrison drove to the Amtrak train station using Google Maps to give him their signature dark-blue line from the Petro Shopping Center. It was an easy eight-mile drive. He parked in the Hoefgen parking lot behind the train station and waited for his asshole brother's train. The only time he got out was to tie a red bandana to the radio aerial. It turned out to be a five-hour wait.

The Amtrak diesel pulled into the station blowing its horn and rattling down the track at 6:15 in the morning. Garrison got up off the unmade bed, put on a Levis jacket, and walked to the little built-in table at the front of the Trek. He'd parked sideways toward the front entrance to the station so Gil couldn't miss the big yellow and tan box. He left the parking lights on. A few minutes later, his text bell dinged. "Gare. In the Amtrak Station. Where are U? Gil."

Dumb shit, Garrison thought. We haven't seen one another for ten years and he can't follow directions? He texted back. "I am in south parking lot. Come out double door. See Yellow TREK RV. Running lights on. Red bandanna on aerial."

A minute later, the station door opened and a roller-bag man stopped under the overhead light. The parking lot was well lit and he could see the tall man dressed in black.

He flicked the interior lights on and off. The man walked toward him, slowly as though he was on the lookout. *Just like always*, Garrison thought. *He's thinking he's the big brother and I need him.*

Garrison stood up, opened the door, and stepped down onto the aluminum plate and from there to the asphalt. Keeping his jaw locked tight, he waited as his brother dragged the noisy roller bag toward him.

"By the light of the Lord God Jesus," Gilbert said, "we are together once again."

He hurried forward, letting go of the handle, and stretched both arms wide. Gilbert embraced Garrison for way too long, hugging him and mumbling something. Garrison was perplexed for a few seconds before realizing his brother was speaking Latin. *A goddamn prayer*, he thought.

Once back inside the RV, Garrison said, "Well, brother, I hope you know I would not have involved you in the mess I'm in except that I have nowhere else to turn."

Those words worked just as they always had. From the time they could talk, his brother had tried to control everything in their lives. Even now, standing inside the poorly lit RV, he sensed Gilbert's deep-seated need to dominate and be *the goddamn big brother*. Gilbert began his preachy way to prove how little he'd changed in the last ten years.

"Garrison, Garrison, my God, let me look at you. You look too thin, and pallid. Me? I'm too fat. It's all that church food, you know."

"Gilbert, now that I look at you, you're right. You're always right. We have the same face, but I'm taller and you're a little heavier. What do you weigh?"

"I'm sad to say I'm 201. You?"

"One eighty five back in Phoenix. But I've probably put on a few pounds since I've been on the road for almost two weeks now. Eating junk food. Speaking of which, I bought your breakfast. There on the table—a foot-long salami sandwich—mayo—no lettuce—and a bag of corn chips. Wanna eat it now, or would you rather drive up the road? I saw an I-Hop a few miles back up on the I-10."

"No, brother. Please, let's just sit. I had coffee and doughnuts for dinner last night. Tell me what's wrong."

Garrison had been rehearsing his cover story for a full day now. He had it in his head, but now that he was facing his brother, three feet away across the Formica table, he had trouble finding the words.

"Well, it's embarrassing to have to tell you brother, especially since we have not been on good terms for a long time, but here's the nub of it. I am being chased by my former employer. She's a sick woman, mentally I mean. She's rich and got that way by embezzling money from her own company. I found out too late, even though she hired me as the company's first comptroller several months ago. And . . ."

Gilbert interrupted. "Have you gone to the police about this?"

"No, of course not. See, that's the reason she hired me in the first place. She set me up to take the blame! Me! I know you can't imagine that. But here I am. Running for my life—with her private investigators following me and hoping I'll make a mistake. Then they will conduct some kind of citizen's arrest, but they won't take me to jail. They will murder me and then say they did it in self-defense because I have a gun and, well, I don't know how exactly, but I know they are out there. I can feel it."

"You have a gun? I just can't imagine you with a gun. How do you know all this, Gare? I mean it sounds fantastical. We last talked on the phone when you were in Scottsdale and, well, you sounded sort of upset, but nothing like this. Are you sure someone is looking for you?"

"You goddamn bet I'm sure. I know who, how, where they are, even right now!"

"Tell me, brother. I don't understand."

Garrison slid out of the booth and went to the little closet between the stove and the back bedroom. He pulled out his Lenovo ThinkPad and brought it back to the table. He turned it on, fingered the local drive, and spun his cover story.

"I know because I have this laptop. You probably won't understand the technology, but I use this to read text messages sent to and from a man named Vince. Well, actually, he isn't a man—he's an alter personality state of a woman. She is my employer, but he takes over and . . ."

"Garrison, wait a sec here. Hold on, I have no idea what you're talking about."

"Right, Gil. It is mindboggling to me too. Don't worry about the technology. Just trust me that I can read Vince's text messages because I used this computer to hack into his cell phone. Once I was inside his cell, I placed a directive that works like a hidden 'cc' program. You know, if you text someone, you can also send that text at the same moment to someone else. It comes from the old typewriter days—cc means carbon copy. No matter. Just believe me when I say

Vince has hired a man named 'Clatch' and they know I met a woman named 'Sharon' two days ago in Houston. She told them about this RV I'm driving, and even gave them my cell phone number. They're not here in San Antonio yet, but they're on the way, and when they get here they will kill me. You're my only hope. Help me, Gil. Help me."

"Well, let's get this old buggy out of sight, Garrison. Can they track you here?"

"No, brother, not unless they are hacking my texts to you. Let's both stay off our phones. Meanwhile, I'll tell you my plan for today and tomorrow."

CHAPTER 35

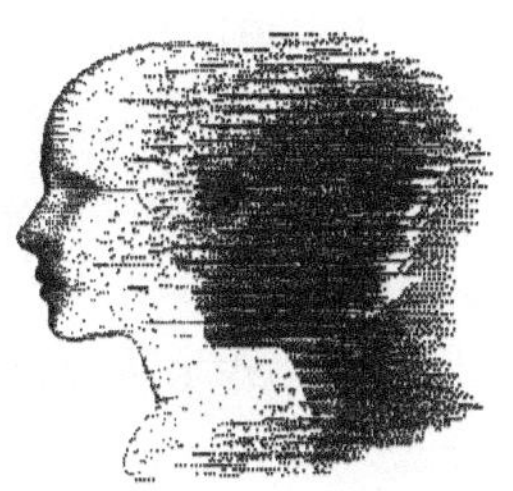

As promised, the Gulfstream IV chartered by Sherlock Sleuths got Vince, Clatch, and two other agents to Signature South San Antonio Airport in just over thirty-seven minutes, wheels up to wheels down. Two chartered Range Rovers with armed drivers were at the taxi gate. There had been no new texts captured during the trip, so Clatch arranged the use of a private conference room at Signature South.

Vince was not happy.

"Well, this is the shits," he said once they were settled in with cold water bottles, note pads, and Signature South ballpoint pens handy. "We're here. You guys believe Garrison is here, somewhere. But nobody knows where. What 'n hell do we do with that?"

Clatch leaned back in his chair and cupped his hands behind his neck.

"Now, Vince, we have to trust more technology. If we were law enforcement we could look at CCTV monitors all over town, but we're not. You know about CCTV surveillance, right? Every city in the country has it. Thousands of private companies use it, all over the country and especially in big cities like San Antonio. Essentially, it uses video cameras to transmit a signal to a specific place on a limited set of monitors. Within the hour we will have a dozen PIs all over town knocking on doors asking to look at video footage. Many will say no, since we're not law enforcement. But many will say yes because our people will say it's a private emergency and we'll pay $250 for a thirty-minute look at what their coverage shows passed by in the last two hours. They all have a photo line-up of the 1994 Safari Trek, both in color and in black and white. They have photocopies of both Venable brothers. And they are looking at coverage in and around truck stops, bus stops, RV parks, and any place they think one or the other Venable brothers might go."

Vince was not happy.

"Freakin' needle-in-haystack shit to me. What if they avoided all the cameras? What's our back-up plan?"

Clatch poured a Styrofoam cup full of black coffee, his tenth in the last few hours.

"Well, Vince, here's the thing about surveillance. People can hide for only so long. At some point they gotta eat, walk around, shit, buy something, sell something, do something suspicious, call someone, or piss in a back alley. It's a process, like netting for fish in a lake. If your net drags over the bottom long enough, you'll catch what you're looking for. Here's how you can help us find Garrison. Tell us more about the man. Can he cocoon himself for a long time, or will hiding out drive him nuts? Is he a patient man, or will he have to act? If we knock on his door will he open the door, or fire a 12-gauge through it at us? I mean, tell us more about his personality. What does he like? What does he hate?"

"Fuck if I know," Vince said defensively. "You guys are the ones always spying on people, right? I don't pay any attention to what people say, about what they like, hate, or who they might kill. People leave me alone, I do my thing, and they don't fuck with me; that's what I want. You ask about his personality. Fuck's that? He's the one that goes around counseling innocent people about their backgrounds, was they happy when nine years old, all that kind of shit!"

Clatch and the other two men in the room sat quietly, not reacting.

Clatch said, "Vince, hey man, sorry to upset you. You're right; we do spy on people. It's in our line of work. And most of the time it's crappy. Why don't you get some air? Walk around the parking lot. Look at the planes. Get your mind off this asshole that's trying to do you and your company great harm."

Vince grabbed his backpack and walked out.

Manuel, the newest guy on the team, asked, "Well, that's not a guy you want in your foxhole when the mortar rounds start dropping. Wow. He's a section-eight for sure. He sounds paranoid to me, just like my ex."

The local team included a man who used to be a railroad detective for the Union Pacific. He used that to talk the security department into giving him a look at the parking lot over the last hour. He promised to buy pizza for the whole crowd for lunch. He watched two camera angles for thirty-eight minutes before he saw the yellow motor home parked sideways in front of the parking lot door. It was just moving out of the lot toward the exit on the north side. Glancing at his stock photo of a Safari Trek, he knew it was the same vehicle.

"Hey man, could you back up this camera for me? I think I see what I'm looking for."

He watched as they slowly rewound the tape backward. He watched it back up, its lights go off, and sit still. Then he saw the driver come out and wait a minute, then another man in a dark suit walked up and embraced the man waiting on the asphalt. They made a copy for him, while he called it in to Clatch.

Once Vince heard the news he banged his fist on the table.

"Hey, you spy guys know your shit, don't you? What do we do now?"

Clatch pointed at the youngest man on the team. "Tell him, Charlie."

"Well, now we know the RV is in town. Your man Garrison was the guy standing by the yellow motorhome, waiting. Our techies played with the tape and think the guy doing the hugging thing was wearing either a white stiff collar or a white turtleneck. Not that clear. But odds are that the motorhome that took a left on Hoefgen Avenue is the one we're looking for and the man you want is at the wheel."

"So, how do we find him from there?"

Clatch answered, "Two ways. First, we have four cars heading up and down I-37, which is right next to the train track. They are getting on and off at every ramp looking for RV parks or places where your man might take a space and hide out again. Second, we're trying to finagle a way to see cameras at every off ramp six miles up and eight miles down. That yellow thirty-foot box on wheels will be easy to spot. But we have to get access to the video. I hate to say it again, but we're not law enforcement so we have to buy our way in."

"You're sure he's here," Vince drawled. "So, how long will it take for all your resources to find that yellow box?"

"Could be within the hour. Could be two-three days. Your man isn't using his cell now. Maybe he smells us. I booked rooms for us at the Marriot next to the Alamo. Maybe your guy is a history buff and we'll find him there, making his last stand."

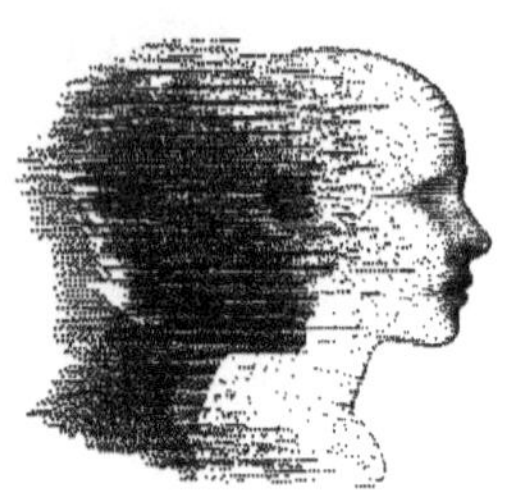 CHAPTER 36

Garrison and Gilbert settled into the two front seats facing the four-foot-square double windshields. He could still hear that clicktey-clack sound from the engine well.

"What's that engine noise?" Gilbert asked.

"Hey, man I dunno. I just bought this giant hunk of steel and aluminum a week ago. Do you know anything about engines? Something maybe you learned in the seminary?"

"No, little brother, we didn't drive in the seminary. But since I've been in New Mexico and have been driving mostly used cars, I've learned a little about bad engine sounds. Sounds to me like you got a lifter problem. It won't stop the engine from running. Most New Mexicans just turn up the volume on the radio. How's the oil drum? You checked it lately?"

"Nah, when I was in Australia, nobody had lifter problems, whatever that is. But now that we're on the road, let me tell you about this RV. In Safari talk, they call the passenger seat you're in the 'copilot' seat. That's a good name, don't you think? You're now my copilot. I'm the pilot and navigator. So, first thing. Here's our flight plan. We're going to take I-35 exactly 79.5 miles northeast to Austin. We'll spend a half-day there, then leave this old RV in a park or something, catch a cab to the airport, and from there we fly to New Orleans. Ever been to New Orleans?"

"No, but let's come back to the travel plans in a minute. Tell me the truth, why are they hunting you?"

"Gil, you know what a whistle blower is, don't you?"

"I don't read newspapers or watch much TV, but I think you're talking about people who discover frauds or thefts from the government, right?"

"Yes, that's it. Whistle blowers sometimes get involved with tax frauds and schemes to evade taxes. My former employer, a company called Emergence Incorporated, committed tax fraud on a grand scale. They have been cheating on taxes for two years, at least. I discovered what they did about a month ago. I had their financial records, but it was buried pretty deep. Anyhow, I was getting ready to blow the whistle on them when they fired me. That was a mistake. They should have killed me when they had the chance, back in Phoenix. That's why they're after me now, in Texas."

Gilbert's mouth went slack and he rubbed one eyelid.

"But Gare, what difference does driving all the way across New Mexico and half of Texas make? No matter how far you drive, won't they eventually find you? They must be rich. They can hire trackers and detectives, right?"

Garrison's stomach growled. *You never quit, do you!* Taking in a deep breath, he tried to dispel his brother's reasoning.

"Gil, I drove across Arizona to New Mexico because I knew if I flew, there would be a record with the airline. Same for the train. So I drove. Only paid cash for gas, food, everything. Never stayed in a hotel. My plan was to contact you earlier, like when I crossed into El Paso, but I was scared and just kept on driving. Finally, in Houston, things happened and I knew they were getting close."

He didn't tell his brother about Sharon or the screw-ups with her. He still hated himself for that.

"OK, Gare, I get that. But why Austin? And why New Orleans? What's there to protect you? And me too? I mean, twin brothers traveling together. Won't that draw a little attention?"

"Maybe, but I needed you. See, I figured out how to get out of the country. You brought your passport, right, like I told you to?"

Gilbert nodded but Garrison could read the tell on his face. *He doesn't believe me, the asshole!*

"I got it mapped out, Gil. I'll show you when we get up to Austin. Like I said, we'll spend the night there. We fly to New Orleans tomorrow morning. There's an 11:40 flight on American we can catch."

"Then what, we fly to the South Pole?"

Because Gil believed he was older, he had always been sarcastic. Garrison was sick of it. *Just keep it up, asshole!*

"Damn, Gil. Give me a little break here, will you? I've traveled all over this country, and Australia. I've even been to Santiago, Chile! You need to trust me on this, OK? In New Orleans, we take the shuttle to the cruise port. There we take a Norwegian Cruise Line seven-day cruise to Jamaica. We get off in Jamaica and stay there for a year or two! Got it? And . . ."

Gilbert slammed both palms down on his thighs. He had not been taking confessions for years, but he remembered how practiced and false most young men were inside the confessional booth. This plan sounded made up. He had acquired the practiced ear priests use to detect false witnesses to God's grace.

"Just you wait a minute, Gare. I came running when you called. I even brought my passport, but I didn't know why. Now you say we're going to fly from Austin to New Orleans, get on a cruise ship, and end up in Jamaica. You need to slow down. I have responsibilities at the monastery. I could be away for a month, maybe, but any more than that and I would be unfaithful to my mission and my scholarly work in the name of our Lord Jesus. So . . ."

It was Garrison's turn to interrupt and act disappointed.

"Gilbert, you're not listening, are you? I need you to travel with me because I feel safer that way. No one will bother us because you're a priest and people will respect your privacy, what with your monastery gig and all. We'll be masked and I'll also be bandaged. We won't look like brothers. Just hear me out, that's all I ask. Let's say you only stay in Jamaica a week or two. I'm paying for all the travel expenses and hotels and everything! I'll buy you a first-class plane ticket from Jamaica back to El Paso whenever you say you want to come back. By then we probably won't be on speaking terms anyway, the way we're starting out. Come on, big brother, you can do this for me can't you?"

CHAPTER 37

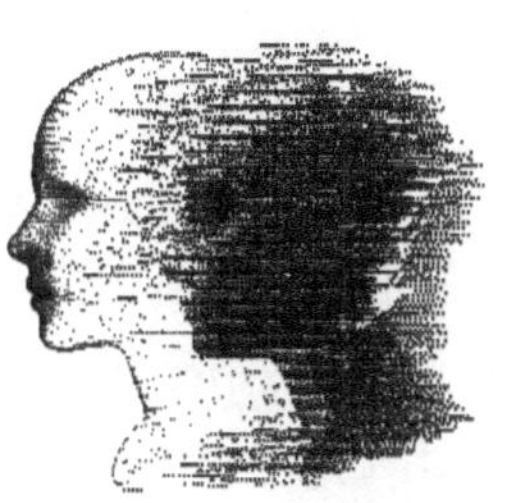

Austin was a big city and the capital city, but it would work out just fine, Garrison thought. *Just you wait, Gilbert.*

They stopped for gas and a late lunch at a truck stop on the outskirts of Austin, wearing their masks from the parking lot to the little restaurant next door. Not everyone inside had a mask, except for the waitress and the short-order cook. Garrison slid his iPad across the Formica to Gil. "Take a look at the airport with this. You'll see there's a big city park close by. It looks like a good place for us to spend the night."

Gil knew how to use Google on a computer but had never used an iPad. He seemed amazed at the touch screen technology. They found a place where they could park the trailer for the night. It was called McKinney Falls State Park. On the satellite map it looked like maybe a thirty-minute walk from there to Austin-Bergstrom International

Airport. Garrison said they'd leave the keys in the ignition and maybe some deserving homeless guy would find it and live in it for the rest of his life.

Gilbert said, "With the good Lord willing."

It was dark by the time they got there. They drove into the park and saw walking trails and some activity, but not much. A half mile in they saw the sign: *Upper McKinney Falls Parking*. It said no overnight parking but Garrison said it didn't matter. There were two other RVs close together about a quarter mile away. They picked the last spot facing Onion Creek. Garrison said he'd treat his favorite brother to a fine dinner—Spam over red beans, with canned spinach and Coors Lite to wash it down. To his surprise, Gilbert said he hadn't had Spam for years, but recalled them getting it as little kids in New York.

Garrison parked, showed Gilbert which of the twin beds he'd be using that night, and popped open two cans of Coors. He poured both into beer steins some former owner had left behind. They were perfect, Garrison thought. Dark glass with a faded logo. He worried whether Gilbert would drink two full mugs.

"Let's get a little drunk, Gil. We haven't done that for, what, maybe a dozen years ago?"

"More 'n that, little brother. So, you're a beer man now, are you? Somehow I figured you'd be a wine drinker, what with your graduate degree and all."

"I drink wine, but only in female company. When I'm with the boys, I still chug beer with the best of 'em. You? Still a beer drinker?"

"Yeah, even though the pastor frowns on it. Not the Lord's drink, he says."

They had one before dinner and another with the salty Spam and the overcooked spinach.

Garrison said, "Let's move from the table to the club chairs—they're comfy. And this bench is getting hard. I'll pour us a Coors' nightcap and we'll stumble back to our twin beds. That's a joke, right—twins sleeping in twin beds after two beers. Way to go, Gil."

Garrison went back to the rear while Gil settled in the club chair behind the copilot seat he'd been in all day.

"Hey, Gare," Gil said, "this club chair has a seat belt too. Should we buckle up for this last beer?" He laughed at his little joke.

Garrison said, over his shoulder, "That's right, big brother, buckle up."

Gil could not see the rear bedroom from his club chair. He didn't see Garrison pull his canvas gym bag out from under the bed. Garrison opened the bag and fished out the small white plastic pillbox with the two mashed Xanax pills, now in powder form. He stuck it in his shirt pocket. Walking back to the front he stopped at the little fridge and got two more beers. He set the two mugs in the drain board next to the sink, where Gil couldn't see. He poured the white power into the bottom of Gil's mug, then poured the can of Coors into it and swirled it with a dirty spoon from the sink. He poured the other beer into his own mug and carried both back to the club chairs.

He could hardly believe his luck. Gilbert smiled, nodding down at the seat belt clipped across his lap and chest.

Garrison smiled back, "Hey Bro, you are a safe traveler aren't you, all buckled up? Good idea. We might hit a bump or two while you're drinking your last beer."

 He handed Gil's stein to him and sat in the other chair.

Garrison toasted, "To life on the run."

Gil toasted back, "To a fine little brother who finally figured his big brother does love him."

They didn't talk but just sat, sipped their beers, and enjoyed the night sounds coming in from the creek. It took about ten minutes for Gil to empty his stein. In another minute the Xanax did its job. Father Gilbert was nearly unconscious, but held in place by his seat belt.

Garrison got up and checked Gil's pulse. It was weak, but present. He shook his brother lightly by the shoulders. He seemed to try to talk. His eyelids were closed and his body was slumped forward in the club chair.

With Gil limp, Garrison bent down and took off his brother's shoes and socks. Then, he unbuckled his belt, unzipped his pants, and lifted him up enough to get his pants off. Next, he took Gil's shirt and clerical collar off. He wore an A undershirt and a scapular. Garrison hadn't seen one since they were little kids. It was a two half-inch-wide small rectangular stiff piece of cardboard, one hanging on the chest and the other on the upper back, strung on black cloth string. It had that Catholic feel to it. He remembered they called it a scapular. He took it off and hung it around his own neck.

Then he took off his own clothes in reverse order. First his T-shirt with the kangaroo images, then his shoes and socks. Last, he took off his belt and pants. Everything in his pockets stayed in place. It was harder than he'd thought it would be, dressing an unconscious man, but in five minutes he had that part finished, including replacing the seat belt and using it to hold Gil's upper body in place.

As quickly as he could, he put on Gil's clothes, including his wallet and pocket change. He left his own wallet, handkerchief, and pocket stuff in the Levis he'd just put on Gil. He'd barely finished when he heard Gil's stomach gurgle and saw his eyes flutter. He seemed to be trying move his arms, but couldn't. He made throat sounds, but not words.

Taking long steps, he went back, pulled Gil's roller bag off the bed, and carried it back to the front. Next, he got his own canvas gym bag and fished inside for the stubby Taurus .357 Magnum. Flipping open the chamber, he took the four bullets out, one by one, holding each bullet firmly between his right thumb and forefinger. He reloaded the gun, cocked it, and laid it on the floor next to Gilbert's right foot.

Gil's shirt was too big, and his black shiny shoes needed two pairs of socks before he tied the laces. He had trouble attaching the clerical collar, but it finally clipped around his neck. It was too loose, but it would do its job, Garrison thought.

He had no idea how long he had before Gil would come out of his stupor. He grabbed a rag and a bottle of cleaning solvent and wiped off each surface he knew Gil had touched inside the RV. He'd been careful to open and close the door himself. His own prints were firmly planted on the bullets, the gun handle, and the small trigger. They would match every surface that Garrison had touched in the last week. He wiped Gilbert's prints off the chair, front seat area, dinner utensils, and the beer glass now sitting in the sink. He washed and dried his own utensils and put them in the drawer.

Garrison left all his stuff in drawers, including his shaving kit, one prescription with his name on the label, and vitamins. He stuck the vial of Xanax and the envelope with a little over seven thousand dollars in the inside pocket on the jacket Gil had worn but that was now on him. He slid the briefcase out from under the bed containing his cruise line documents, fake passport, and a new toothbrush, toothpaste, plastic razor, and a small flashlight. They were hidden in the false bottom it had taken him a full day to sew into place. He stuffed the canvas bag into the roller bag and rolled it to the door. Last, and most important, he took Gilbert's US passport and shoved it down into his pants pocket.

Opening the side door, he watched the automatic step slide out. Stepping quickly down, he walked all the way around the Trek, making sure no one was around. A dim light was on in one of the RVs parked a quarter mile away. As he stood there, the lights in the other RV seemed to flicker, but he didn't hear any sounds from that direction. He went back in, got Gilbert's roller bag, and wheeled it out onto the gravel. Outside, the night air was still and the only sound he heard was the creek gurgling forty feet on the other side of his RV.

Shaking his head forward and back, and steeling himself, he stepped back up and into the RV. His brother was stirring. Feeling the need, he made the sign of the cross on his forehead and both shoulders. Then he picked up the .357 from the floor, making sure to hold gun firmly in his right hand. He used his left hand to open Gilbert's mouth and tip his head back onto the top of the chair. Then, exhaling and gritting his teeth, he stuck the stubby little two-inch barrel in his brother's mouth. Leaning back as far as he could, he pulled the trigger.

The boom was deafening inside the closed confines of the trailer. Blood, tissue, and brain matter spewed backward and up over the club chair, the copilot's chair, and half of the driving compartment. Gilbert's right arm hung limply almost to the floor. Garrison moved it back up to his brother's lap. Then he placed the gun carefully in his dead brother's hand. The barrel felt hot. Garrison felt faint, but shook it off.

He stepped down to the ground, closed the door, and carried the bag across the gravel to the asphalt roadway. Lights came on in the other RV to his left. He put the roller bag down on the road and jogged up the asphalt roadway and around the curve. The night air seemed chilled but he kept going, getting more than a football field away, through two curves and a slight uphill pull before he heard sirens in the distance. Leaving the paved roadway, he used his small flashlight to find the walking path from the parking lot to the entrance to McKinney Falls State Park. The opening in the fence along the roadway was a welcome sight. It led across the walking part of the park and to the other side, where he saw the first police car careen around the far curve and turn left into the park. He walked quickly, but worried about looking too obvious to the few cars that passed him. In a half hour, he was at the airport, and out of breath.

CHAPTER 38 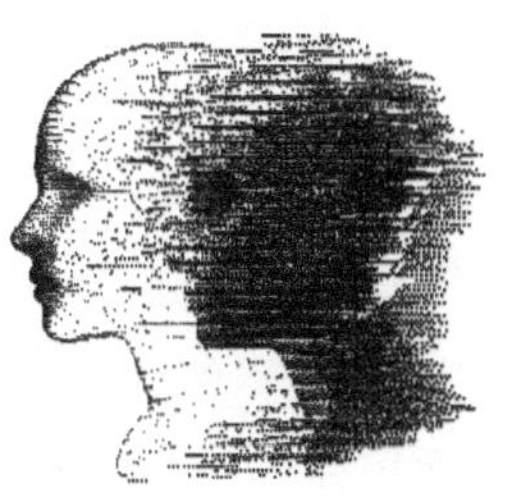

Vince had been asleep on top of the blankets on his hotel bed when his cell phone buzzed and made a scratching noise on the fake wood table next to the bed. His head hurt from the bourbon Clatch had insisted they have in the hotel bar, alongside well-done rib eye steaks, green beans, and ice cream for dessert. He looked at the ever-present electric phone—it glared in white graphic letters "**4:11 A.M.**"

"OK," he said, "what you got?"

Clatch said, "Vince, the hunt is over. Your man offed himself last night in Austin."

"Clatch, you can't be saying what I think you're saying," Vince gurgled. His mouth tasted like sandpaper and his head throbbed. "Fuck's this? Offed himself! Hung himself, jumped off a bridge, whadda ya saying, Clatch?"

"I'm saying Garrison Venable committed suicide last night, around ten o'clock. First police reports said the 911 calls came in at 9:10 p.m. in a public park. He was inside the Safari Trek we've been chasing for two days. Two fucking days!"

"How come you're just now calling me and this happened yesterday?"

"Well, Austin police went hot on a 911 call about a gun shot. A single gunshot. Some lady in a different RV called it in. She wasn't hysterical or anything. The first unit on the scene didn't know whether it was a misfire, or even if someone was hurt. The lights inside the RV were on, but they didn't see anyone inside. This is what our agent in Austin said. They knocked on the door, no answer, but the lights were on inside. They looked through the front windshield and saw a man slumped over in a chair inside. Then they found him."

"You're saying Garrison shot himself? What was he thinking, doing something like that?"

"Vince, it's bad. He put a .357 Magnum in his mouth and blew half his head off. The EMT told our agent it was a bloody mess. Brain matter, skull bones, skin, and hair, all over the driver's compartment, even on the ceiling. It'll take a long day to get it all straight. Question is, do you wanna go there, or take the cop's word? The driver's license in his wallet and the morgue photo confirm the victim as Garrison Venable. His finger prints are on the gun and all over the RV."

"You crazy or what!" Vince screamed. "Fuckin' right I want to go there. I got to see his body today."

Clatch said he'd book a helicopter and call back when the car was ready to take them to the heliport on the other side of town. They got to Austin before lunch. The medical examiner was not through with the body until four that afternoon. Clatch argued his client had a right to see the body because he was a key employee and had been under great stress for several weeks. Once they got inside the cold room, and the attendant in the white jacket and trousers pulled out the body on a standard morgue stretcher, Clatch felt shaky. He was used to chasing people, but dead bodies were rare in his part of the PI world.

Fortunately, Vince's insistence on seeing the body was short-lived. The attendant unzipped the white nylon bag and opened it wide enough so Vince could see the body from the chest up. There was no blood on the face, his eyes were taped over, and the skull area was covered by what looked like polypropylene layered over gray packing material. Vince threw up, so they hustled him out into the hallway and towards the men's room.

Back in the Range Rover, Clatch said, "Let's just talk here, Vince. The medical examiner is going to define this as a suicide. There's no crime here. The bullet from his gun was found in the hard metal dashboard. His DNA will be tested, as well as his blood and other organs. But from everything we know now, this is the end of the chase. Your bad guy is dead. I'll shut down the Texas search protocol and . . ."

"No, goddamnit, no!"

Clatch could see what looked like foam spilling out of Vince's mouth. Clatch had only seen this once and that was on a rabid dog he'd seen years ago.

"Clatch, you better listen to me on this. Our company has already paid you a pile of money and we're still under contract. You have to figure out what really happened inside that shitty yellow trailer. Won't the cops have to write a report? They gotta investigate, right?"

"Vince, this is Texas, a died-in-the-wool gun state. Most people here have guns and hundreds of Texans get shot every year. Hell, man, I even did a quick state search while I was waiting for confirmation on the helicopter rental this morning. The Austin Police Department did a study last year on gun violence in the city. They looked at all kinds of gun deaths. Suicide, criminal homicides, nonfatal shootings, domestic violence involving firearms, and mass shootings. Can you guess which category was not an issue with them?"

"What do you mean, 'an issue'?"

"I mean which kind gun violence was of no interest to the police?"

"How n' hell would I know? I ain't a cop."

"Exactly, Vince. Neither are we. We are private investigators. We've handled thousands of cases over the last six and a half years, but no one has ever asked us to investigate a suicide. No one has ever asked a police department, even the FBI to investigate a suicide. It's not a crime to off yourself. It could be a crime to help someone else do it, but you and your company can't possibly want us to look into that."

"Well shit fire, Clatch. How do we know for sure it was a suicide? Maybe someone broke in to rob Garrison, and then shot him for the hell of it! They gotta look into that, right?"

"Sure, Vince. That determination, whether it was a suicide or a homicide, will be done by the medical examiner in

Travis county. I took a quick look at their jurisdiction this morning. Their website says they provide medico-legal death investigation for Travis County and a half-dozen surrounding counties. There are over a million people under their jurisdiction. I made notes. Let me read the most important one to you, quote, 'Forensic medical examiners investigate deaths, perform crime scene investigations, collect evidence, and develop decedents' medical and social histories to assist the medical examiner in determining the cause and manner of death.'"

Vince looked perplexed. Clatch had been trying for days to understand what made Vince tick. He decided he'd grown up in a secluded society where knowledge of the wider world was limited.

"So, you're saying we have to wait until the Texas mortician guys decide? That's what you're saying?"

"I'm saying that the medical examiner for this county is legally charged with the duty to issue a report and a death certificate that will state the cause of death. They will look for evidence of homicide. They have clear evidence already of suicide, but they will have to rule out homicide. If their investigation confirms what the first responders thought, then there is nothing more to investigate. I hate to say it, but you hired us to find Garrison Venable. We did that. You and I saw him on a mortuary stretcher today. You are asking the right question. Did he commit suicide or did someone kill him? We cannot investigate that. No outside agency could. Your question will be answered, but it will take a long time."

"Why's that? I mean, shit, they have the gun, right? You told me that. They have the bullet and can match it up, like I see on TV, right? Why will it take a long time?"

"Because they have to test DNA, blood, and urine for drugs or infections. They say no two bodies are alike once they get to the ME's office. But in time, they will issue a death certificate and a report will be filed. If it's suicide, they close the investigation. If it's homicide, the police will gear up. Either way, I'll keep tabs and let you know the instant the death certificate is ready. Meanwhile, Vince, you should go home."

"Well, this is double fucked, ain't it? Next you're gonna tell me we have to pay what's her name, Sharon, the twenty-five thousand dollar reward. Is that right?"

"Yes, of course. She gave us the essential information that led us to Austin. We found your missing man—Mr. Garrison Venable—well, at least we found his body."

They drove from the ME's office to the Austin-Bergstrom International Airport and dropped Vince off. Southwest Airlines had a plane only half-full that would make two stops before reaching Phoenix. It would leave in four hours. Vince would bide his time in the Southwest gate area.

CHAPTER 39

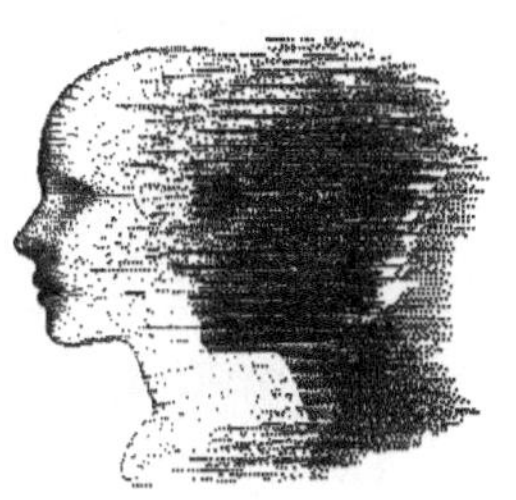

While neither had the slightest inkling of proximity, Vince and Garrison were in the same building-complex, the Barbara Jordan Terminal, that afternoon. Vince bought his Southwest Airlines ticket at the east ticket counters and waited at Gate 2 for his trip to Phoenix.

Garrison, wearing a clerical collar, a black suit, and well-shined shoes, bought his ticket at the west ticket counters. After paying cash for an economy-class ticket to London, he went through the TSA line with Gilbert Venable's passport. He waited near the international passengers lounge at Gate 21 for his departure to London.

Vince landed in Phoenix five hours later, Mountain Standard Time. Garrison landed in London the next morning at 9:40 a.m. Greenwich Mean Time. Vince used his flight time to stab mental wounds into Garrison. Garrison used his seven-hour flight to study a book he'd found in the Austin airport books and newspaper store. The title alone excited him: *The Walk of a Lifetime: 500 Miles on the Camino de Santiago.* He wondered whether the COVID-19 pandemic in Europe would close down the pilgrimage. *Hope not—sounds like a great place to hide while the fools in Austin fuck around with Gilbert's body, thinking it's me!*

Vince deplaned in Phoenix, caught a Lyft ride to Desert Mountain, and went in the side gate to the casita in back. He dropped his backpack on the floor and went across the pool to the master bedroom in the main house.

Thirty minutes later, Vinessa woke up, took off her grungy travel clothes, showered, and put on a long-sleeved cashmere sweater over her Veronica Beard wide-length pants and her new Tory Burch flat Espadrilles. She was ravenous and began thawing a sushi-grade ahi tuna steak and mixing a kale salad.

Garrison, feeling comfortable as "Father Gilbert," checked into the YotelAir Hotel located inside London's Heathrow International Airport. It was, as the brochure in the seatback pocket said, "Conveniently located in the public landside area of Terminal 4, on the mezzanine level. We're only minutes away from the departure and arrival gates." He spent twelve hours there, making travel arrangements to Pamplona, Spain, for his five-hundred-mile trek across the Pyrenees in France and then spilling over into Spain. He had no religious interest in ever getting to the shrine of the apostle Saint James the Great. But as a goal, the Cathedral of Santiago de Compostela made sense. It was a way to hide in plain sight with thousands of pilgrims retreating for spiritual growth. No one at the airport seemed to know whether Spain was still welcoming American priests during their crackdown because of the pandemic.

From Spain, Garrison sent a text to Gilbert's monastery in Hobbs, New Mexico.

Father Espinoza. Forgive me father, for I have sinned. I am in Spain making the pilgrimage for God and his son, our Lord Jesus Christ. It will take me as far as God wants me to go. Yours in Christ, Father Gilbert Venable.

Garrison was never athletic, and the pandemic had virtually shut down pilgrims following the famous yellow arrows leading the way to Santiago de Compostela. But he enjoyed moving from one Spanish three-star hotel to another. Everything connected with the pandemic, from masks to sheltering in place, suited him. Two months later, from Madrid, he flew to Jamaica using his fake Jamaican passport. It worked just fine.

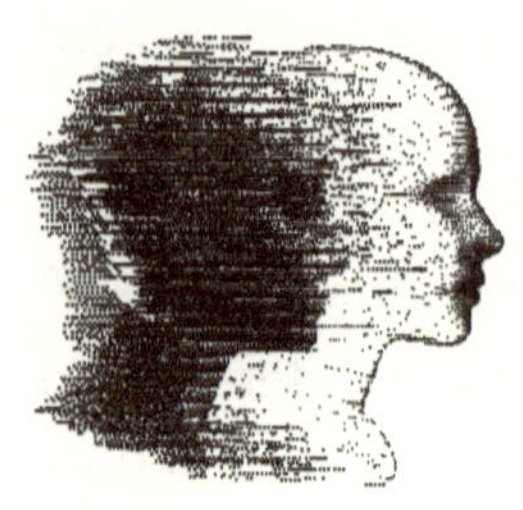

CHAPTER 40

A month after Vince came home from Austin, Vinessa wrote a short note to each family whose money had been embezzled by Garrison Venable.

Dearest family member of Emergence Incorporated,

It is with a broken heart but a settled mind that I send this note. We have experienced a financial disappointment in carrying out the Family Trust Agreement program due to the tragic death of our former comptroller, Mr. Garrison Venable. We will be sending each family a certified check for all funds transferred by wire to us last month. Additionally, you will be receiving a signed cancellation of all trust financial

obligations on your part. We hope to
continue our other ongoing member services
with you.

Fondest regards,

Vinessa

Four days later, Vinessa was surprised to get a registered letter from Sherlock Sleuths, LLC, in Dallas, Texas. Inside the stiff envelope, she found the official *Certificate of Death—Garrison Venable—Address Unknown*. It defined his cause of death as, "Cause of death—Suicide—Self-Inflicted—Intentional." The report was a model of clinical assessment, but said nothing about what evidence supported the final determination. There was no mention of a suicide note, mental status, provocation, assistance by others, or moral turpitude. She wondered why there was no mention of Garrison's twin brother, the priest from New Mexico.

Somewhere in her memory, in a time she could not exactly recall, she'd learned that Garrison and another man, presumably his brother Gilbert, had been seen together in San Antonio. Why then, she wondered, was no one looking for the twin brother named Gilbert? Yes, Garrison had committed suicide. The death certificate resolved that. But what about his twin, Father Gilbert? Where was he? Could he be helpful in solving Emergence Incorporated's unanswered question—where were the millions of dollars Garrison stole?

A business card bearing the name of Clayton Unswor was paper-clipped to the death certificate. His Dallas, Texas, office number was listed, along with his cell. She dialed the cell number. She got a message, "This is Clatch. Sorry I don't recognize your number. Please call my office."

She called the office, asked for Mr. Unswor, and was routed to an assistant. The female assistant asked for the case number. Vinessa said she didn't know, but "My brother Vince retained your company on a recent matter."

Five minutes later, her cell rang. She answered with a soft, "Yes."

"Hello, I'm Clayton Unswor, but call me Clatch. Everyone does. Are you related to Vince?" the caller asked.

Vinessa said, "You could say that. I believe Vince retained your office to help him find our former comptroller, Garrison Venable. Were you in charge of that matter?"

"Yes, ma'am, I was. I got to know Vince a little. I sent the death certificate to an address he gave me in Phoenix."

"Yes, I got it and your business card too."

"How can I help you?"

"You can investigate the issue still unresolved, Mr. Clatch."

"It's just Clatch, ma'am. Vince retained us to find Garrison Venable. Sadly, we found him, but only after his death. What unresolved matter is left, if I may ask?"

Vinessa took a deep breath, "Well, I was hoping it would be obvious. I want you to find Fr. Gilbert Venable. I think he *is* Garrison. Can you do that?"

The End